The WITCH with the
TRIDENT TATTOO

Diana McCollum

PLUS
BONUS
STORY

The CRYSTAL WITCH

Diana McCollum

Windtree Press Hillsboro, OR

https://windtreepress.com/

Windtree Press--Publisher
Hillsboro, OR
http://windtreepress.com

Note: These are works of fiction. Names, characters, places, and incidents are a product of the authors' imaginations. Locales and public names are sometimes used for atmospheric purposes. Any resemblance to actual people, living or dead, or to businesses, companies, events, institutions, or locales is completely coincidental or with the express approval of the business, company.

ISBN: 978-1947983021

Book Cover: Karen Duvall
http://duvalldesign.wordpress.com/book-cover-design/
Editor: Kelly Schaub

Dedication

To Family, to friends, and to the Bend writers,

Thank you for your support!

And to Jacques Cousteau, whose fabulous documentaries on the seas were my introduction to the beauty found in the depth of the oceans.

"The sea, once it casts its spell,

holds one in its net of wonder forever."

-Jacques Cousteau-

Chapter One

The town meeting last night had left a bitter taste of disappointment in Ella Stone's mouth. She had tried to convince the upstanding citizens of Waxing, Massachusetts the importance of suspending fishing for twenty square miles off the coast, and inland to Turtle Point and the beach in town. She also suggested no swimming for a couple of weeks while she researched the unknown carbon-based matter depleting the nutrients necessary for sea life to be sustainable. They had rejected her proposal and it had stung, and still stung.

The fishermen needed to make a living, she understood. If they continued to fish and toxic organic matter continued to grow, fisheries would be depleted in a short time. Not to mention she couldn't be sure if the organic material was toxic to humans or not, it was too early in her research to tell.

Arriving for her Saturday shift at her friend Hettie's gift shop, The Crystal Witch, Ella seethed with fury. Her pulse beat a fast tempo, sending an edgy, twitchy feeling over her skin. She marched down the aisle of scented soaps and candles toward the back of the store, as sparks of pent-up Magick flew off her. Wicks on the table of colorful display candles burst into flames as soon as she passed. She breezed by the rack of wind chimes and they tinkled and rattled as if a gust of wind blew through the store when none did.

"Ella, what's the matter?" Hettie Wynn stood in the office doorway, hands wrapped around a cup of coffee.

Ella handed the local newspaper, *Lighthouse News,* to Hettie. "The meeting last night was a bust. Apparently, I am a crazy woman scientist who doesn't know what she's talking about. Wait, no— 'environmental whacko' is what they said."

"I've got a degree in marine biology and oceanography from Salem State University. I've studied under some of the most prestigious professors, and they call me an 'environmental whacko'?" Ella removed her sunglasses and used the edge of her sweater to clean the lenses.

"Did you present your findings in terms they could understand?" Hettie reached out and steadied the wind chime rack.

Ella walked over and blew out candles one by one. In so doing, she blew sample herbal powder out of the display bowl and covered the floor in many colors of powder. She harrumphed at her blunder and crossed her arms. "Sorry for being in such a dither, but you know what I'm up against."

"Poseidon."

"Yes! He wants answers, and only from me. 'What happens in the ocean is a matter for the realm to manage. I'm depending on you to find the answer. Do not involve the human governments.' He's such a pretentious monarch, always playing games with me." Unshed tears of frustration threatened to spill over.

"These waters have been in the care of my family since my ancestors first stepped on shore at Plymouth. There's never been *anything* of this magnitude, *anything* capable of destroying marine plant and animal life to this degree. Whatever has damaged the flora and fauna hasn't reached the shore, but I'm concerned because it's just a matter of time till it does. I've named the toxin Razor Toxic Bloom-RTB-1, and it is spreading past the outer banks toward Waxing."

Ella stalked over to the screened back door. A slice of the ocean was visible from here, sandwiched between two cottages across the alley, an early May breeze blew across her face. Something was invading the waters of *her* ocean. Her mother before her had been the sea witch in charge of taking care of these coastal waters. Ella had inherited the position when her mother and father were called by Poseidon to protect the Bering Sea. "Time is of the essence. Poseidon doesn't want government agencies involved, or other marine biologists. He's got his reasons for believing an immortal is responsible. This problem is for me to solve and time is running out. Whatever RTB-1 is will reach our shore eventually, if not stopped."

She crossed her arms over her chest and turned back to Hettie. "Commercial fishermen protested the loudest, and I understand fishing is their livelihood. But if fish are unhealthy, should anyone be eating them? All the mothers agreed to not let their kids swim or wade for two weeks."

"Do you think you can find an answer by then?"

"I don't know. I hope so." Her stomach clenched. "Do you think what's happening in the ocean is something our coven should look into?"

Hettie walked closer and put her arm around Ella. "I think you need to call on your resources. You are a Sea Witch, none of us are. We can help you on land, but water is your domain. Have you contacted James? Or Mischell? Maybe one of them could do some investigating for you?"

"You're right. Of course, I'll contact James." A fluttering in her chest made her realize she wasn't alone. She had her familiar, James the octopus—the Coastal Coven and her laboratory. She'd find the answer.

"Can I take an early break and contact James? I need him to start working on this problem right away."

"Of course." Hettie smiled and patted Ella on the arm. "Take all the time you need. I have a few errands to run, but they can wait."

# # #

Ten minutes later seated on a rock at the seashore, Ella faced the ocean a light gust of air blew her hair back off her face. Eyes closed she opened her senses up. She could only hope the giant octopus was close to shore and would hear her telepathic call. His den was near a barren island, Razor Island, a few miles off the coast.

James!

Hard to tell what the fellow had been up to last night. He could very well be curled up in his den sound asleep.

James!

Ella my love, I'm off the end of Turtle Point.

She shaded her eyes against the morning sun and looked toward Turtle Point some three hundred yards away.

Do you see me, darling? I'm waving number three of my tentacles, one and two are sadly sore from moving rocks around to better conceal the path to my dwelling.

Four feet or so of his tentacle popped up out of the water, retreated and popped up again.

Yes, yes I see you. Listen, Poseidon contacted me and I have two weeks to find out what is destroying marine and plant life out near Razor Island. The spread of devastation is growing. Would you play detective and see what all you can find out?

But of course my darling, ah-h-h, a secret agent. I'm excited. No, no, I'm ecstatic. No still not right. Hmm, what am I? Exhilarated that's what I am! You're James Bond of the ocean, at your service, my dear.

Ella laughed out loud. *Thanks, Mr. Bond! I'll be in touch.*

# # #

"I have to make a bank deposit. Would you mind the store till I get back?" Hettie slipped into her green jacket. The color popped against her long, curly raven hair. "Promise I'll bring sweet rolls from Seaside Bakery."

"No problem. I'll tidy up those candles I set on fire and clean up the powder. I'm sorry for that." Ella pulled her hair over her left shoulder and proceeded to braid it.

"Don't worry. It's nothing that can't be cleaned." Hettie waved on her way out the back door.

Ella brought the broom and dustpan from the utility room and began sweeping up powder. She hitched her long skirt up and squatted down to better see the fine particles under the table. The bell over the door rang. "I'll be with you in a minute," she said, finishing her task. Heavy steps on the wooden floor stopped short of where she worked.

As she struggled to rise, a strong hand lifted her up by her elbow. She turned around "Thank...*You*!" She jerked her arm out of his grasp, spilling half the contents of the dustpan. He was the tall, darkly-handsome fisherman from last night's meeting.

His brown eyes, set in an angular face, narrowed. A swath of black curls fell casually onto his forehead. Definitely handsome in a rugged sort of earthy way, she guessed maybe thirty-five years old.

"Well, if it isn't the lady scientist." His words were cool and clear as ice water. He looked her up and down, his eyes sharp and assessing.

From his close scrutiny, heat rose up her neck. "What are you doing here?" What indeed? Noah Drago had been quite outspoken at the meeting the previous evening. And she understood he hadn't fished at all since losing his boat in a raging storm last month. Logically she realized he'd be feeling the pinch of no income. Still, her request was not unreasonable.

"I'm here to buy a gift for my aunt. Is Hettie here?" He glanced around the store.

"You'll have to deal with me. Hettie stepped out for a bit." She lifted her chin, the better to see his face. He was so tall and stood so close. He smelled of the ocean, all salt and sea breeze.

"So you work here?" He made a slight gesture, his right hand encompassing the store.

"Part-time, on weekends, gets me out of my lab." She carried the dustpan to the back and dumped the contents in the garbage, stashed the broom and pan in the utility room. She turned in the doorway and ran into his firm chest. Placing her hands on his chest she pushed. "Personal space, back off."

He swung his wide shoulders to the side, allowing her room to pass, and then followed her to the counter. He retrieved a toothpick from his pocket and stuck it between his lips. "A real scientist wouldn't be working in a gift shop."

She was glad for the glass countertop separating them so she could breathe. "*Really*? Are we going to have this conversation now? I work here because I can get out of my lab and around friends and I enjoy the interaction with clients." She looked pointedly at him. "Most customers." She crossed her arms over her chest, doing her best to stay calm. "I don't want to neglect my friends because I value them."

His face turned ashen.

Aha, she struck a nerve. "What's wrong, Mr. Drago? Do you fish so much you don't have time for any buddies? Last I knew you did not have a boat." The words were out before she could stop them. About the same time she remembered he had lost his boat and mate last month to a rogue wave.

He turned on his heel and stomped out the door.

She sucked in a breath and watched the burly fisherman leave. She sighed. Today wasn't the first time she had spoken without thinking. Regretting her childish response, she picked up a feather duster and went on the hunt for dust bunnies, annoying little creatures. She didn't like dealing with confrontation; this was one of the reasons she preferred the solitude of her lab for most of the week.

# # #

Noah stormed out of the gift shop. Arguing was time-consuming and pointless. The soft-spoken scientist from last night's meeting had a temper. When he walked into Hettie's gift shop he had been in a good mood. Buying a gift for Aunt Delores was a good thing. She had survived another bout of cancer treatment and was planning her wedding.

The slender woman stooping to clean up a spill, her silvery Blonde braid hanging down to her tiny waist, was a picture to behold. He couldn't believe his eyes when she turned around and she was the environmental nut from last night's meeting.

Up close he could see she was pretty, sea-green eyes, porcelain skin and around his age, thirty-five. She topped out at five feet three inches and she was svelte. Another time he might be inclined to pursue her, not now.

She had no idea how a ban on fishing would affect their small community. Or she knew, but didn't care.

He didn't even know her name, damn. *Keep your friends close and your enemies closer. Blew that one!* He ran a hand through his hair and then started walking toward the harbor.

Noah stuffed his hands deep in his pockets. He wrapped his fingers around the chain attached to the St. Christopher medallion Bruce, his first mate, and friend, had given him the day before a rogue wave hit their fishing vessel. Taking the medallion out of his pocket, he slipped the chain over his head and the medal under his shirt. The warm medallion nestled against his chest, a constant reminder of his friend, and the harshness of the ocean.

The harbor seals barking and gulls screeching overhead admonished him to start fishing again. His new boat, The *Mystic Mermaid*, had arrived last week and had yet to make her maiden voyage. She was sleek, clean and sparkly, and he couldn't wait to take her fishing. He missed *Lure of the C,* his old boat, it had character, but he didn't miss the high maintenance cost. He had recently christened her the *Money Pit of the C.*

The insurance check for reimbursement had covered most of his cost for the new boat, leaving him a manageable monthly payment. *Manageable* if he was working. There was the rainy day fund he'd set up through his credit union it would help, but he needed to fish to make a sustainable living. Sea grass swayed in the gentle breeze softening the dunes and edging the path he trod. He reached the dock and headed down to where the *Mystic Mermaid* was moored.

"Ahoy, mate, like your new vessel." Oscar Aldrich, brawny old captain of the fishing vessel *Red Moon,* waved from his boat, docked across from the *Mystic Mermaid's* slip.

"Hey, Oscar, what's new?" The grizzled old sea captain held a special place in Noah's heart. Oscar had stepped up and offered Noah a job until his insurance money came through.

Oscar chewed on his cigar before answering, "Pulled half a load of Mackerel yesterday. Couldn't convince Portuguese Joe to buy them after the meeting last night, hauled my load down the coast to sell." He raised his hat and scratched his gray wiry hair. "Didn't matter to Joe I fished up the coast away from the area Ella told us about. She's a top notch gal and I don't think she'd make statements to dissuade us from fishing unless she had proof to back up what she was saying." His gray eyebrows knitted together to form a solid line. "You thinking of going out?"

"Thinking I might." Noah jumped on deck, unlocked the cabin door and secured the hook to an outside eye. "Probably sleep on it a night or two yet." Thinking of fishing without Bruce, his first mate, gave him an empty feeling in the pit of his stomach. He sat down on the deck bench.

"Just like riding a horse—you fall off you need to get right back on." Oscar removed his soggy unlit cigar he'd gnawed on and stuck it in his pocket. A habit he'd picked up since quitting cigarettes.

"I know." Noah ran a hand through his hair. He popped the top to a beer, held the can out toward Oscar, who declined. Noah shrugged, and then took a long swig. "Still haven't found a mate to go with. Bruce will be a damn hard guy to replace." The nearby rumble of the wave over rock echoed his mood.

Oscar shook a stubby finger at Noah. "I hear the fellow who's marrying our Hettie is looking to get on a boat."

Noah stopped his beer halfway to his mouth. "Evan Wolf? I thought he had a good job driving truck."

"He misses the sea. Says he always worked on boats when he was young. When he was in the Marines too, he'd come down to the docks on leave and bug me till I'd let him go out fishing. Damn fine worker, dependable too."

"Thanks, I'll talk to him." He waved to Oscar and went inside to the galley. He'd rustle up some lunch and make a list of supplies he needed. Except for a can of tuna and half a loaf of bread, his cupboards were bare. He pulled the can opener out of the drawer, opened the can of tuna and prepared a sandwich.

Noah sat down at the table with his lunch. This craft had all the bells and whistles, a brand new galley, bunks, and hi-tech bridge, everything a captain could want. She was a great boat.

He bit into his sandwich, smiling to himself, time to take her out on a maiden voyage.

By evening he had stocked his pantry, cupboards and fridge, fixed a decent meal and decided he'd sleep on board tonight. On deck, he turned his chair to look out at the ocean. The last rays of sun glimmered and danced over waves before it slipped behind the tree-lined western horizon.

He unhooked lines from the cleats and pulled the fenders aboard. He switched on the running-lights and cruised out to a favorite spot in the cove out of the channel. Dropping anchor, he attached a bow line to his permanent buoy. Only half a dozen buoys remained along this harbor shoreline. His buoy was now a part of the harbor masters fleet of floats. His choice was clear. Either share the buoy or it would be removed. Waxing not being a huge tourist draw, he hadn't found a problem sharing with the public, and most of the fishermen preferred the safety of moorage at the dock.

Facing the shore he watched while lights blinked on one at a time, as dusk faded into night. He poured a glass of whiskey then raised his glass toward heaven. "To you, Bruce, best friend and one hell of a fisherman! I'll never forget you, buddy." He downed his drink and poured another.

Moonlight cast the beach in pale light and gentle waves frothed as they caressed the sands. Something moved in the water near the mouth of the cove. Someone was swimming alongside Turtle Point, the rocky outcropping which thrust into the Atlantic at the end of the cove roughly fifty yards away.

Must be the whiskey, he considered; no one would be swimming at this time of night. Turtle point was in darkness and he lost track of the swimmer. Probably flotsam the current brought in. He took another swig of whisky straight from the bottle, polishing it off. He looked again but didn't see any flotsam. Instead, emerging from a shadow at the point was a…sea nymph? She stood on the sand a long gauzy dress, soaking wet, and clinging to her body. She wrung out her long hair streaked through with moon light. Blonde? He wasn't sure.

She was facing the sand dunes more or less forty feet from his boat. Holy shit! Her hair hung down her back pass her waist. Thin wet fabric clung to her curves. His boat rocked and unsteady legs betrayed him. He fell toward the sleeping bag he had spread out on deck. The bottle tipped and rolled across the deck. He got his bearings, sat back on the bench and looked over towards the beach. All he saw was a deserted shoreline.

Later the empty Berkshire Mountain bourbon bottle rolled on each swell as the deck rose and fell with the tide. Noah lay on his sleeping bag looking at the stars and his thoughts turned to the sea nymph. The rocking motion made it hard to keep his eyes open. Finally, he gave up and drifted into a deep sleep.

A long tentacle eased up over the side of the *Mystic Mermaid*. The appendage stretched, undulating like a snake till the tentacle reached Noah. The sucker-laced appendage wrapped around Noah's ankle and drew him close to the side. With precision, the tentacle untied his Nike, removed his shoe, and slithered, shoe and all, back into the ocean.

Chapter Two

Sunday morning Ella rose before dawn, anxious to check on the experiments in her lab. She threw on a long denim dress, seahorses were embroidered around the hem, slipped into clogs, and grabbed a wool sweater and hat to fend off the cool, foggy mist permeating the morning air. The laboratory was silhouetted against the waning moon. The scent of dew-covered pines wafted to her nose and she inhaled the clean smell.

Working a spell to undo a protection charm she'd placed on the door last night, she pushed it open, flipped on overhead lights and secured the door from inside. She was safe in her sanctuary. A blue flame danced under a bubbling flask keeping time to the hiss of the Bunsen burner. No change had occurred, still green in color.

She checked multiple Petri dishes holding the unknown pathogen, RTB-1. Yesterday, unable to make a final determination as to whether the sample was plant-based, bacterium or virus at this point, she decided to grow the segment she'd found in a clump of seaweed. Using a calibrator she determined the sample had grown a tiny bit, but not much.

Ella put on goggles and a lab coat. She snapped on latex gloves. Carrying one of the Petri dishes over to her workstation she grabbed the tiny forceps and held the sample while she cut off a thin slice. Placing the specimen on a slide for analysis, she removed her goggles and studied the sample under the microscope.

Lack of movement suggested the culprit was growing slowly and pathogenic. She filled flasks using distilled water in one, and another using a reactive solution to help determine the chemical makeup of the pathogen.

From past experiments, she knew it would take approximately ten hours for any conclusive findings. Ella sighed.

Sometimes research was a wait and see game. Not like the quick response time portrayed on T.V. crime shows.

Morning sun broke free of the fog and peeked in through narrow horizontal windows along the top of the wall. Time to go to the gift shop, Sundays Hettie always made breakfast and coffee, Ella was told this tradition carried over from when Aunt Bea, Hettie's foster mom, ran the shop. She locked up the lab. Grabbing her canvas purse off the table, keys in hand, she headed out to her old Toyota pickup.

The third time the engine failed to turn over Ella grabbed her cell and punched in Hettie's number.

"Good morning," Hettie said her tone cheerful.

"Hey, I'm going to be a few minutes late. My darn truck won't start again."

"You want me to send Evan over to take a look at your truck?"

"No, I'll ask Oscar after work. He told me next time my truck broke down to call him."

"Okay, we'll see you when you get here." Hettie chuckled. "I guess you've figured out by 'we' I mean Evan and me."

"So, when are you two going to tie the knot?"

There was a long pause before Hettie answered. "There's something I wanted to talk to you about, girl to girl."

Ella tamped down a stab of jealousy. She was happy for her friend, especially after all Hettie had been through, but she was sad for herself. She'd had a few boyfriends over the years, but nothing serious and nothing in twelve months. Moving to Waxing a year ago was going to be a new beginning for her, starting by putting herself out there to meet new people, men *and* women.

She had girlfriends; the Coastal Coven had embraced and welcomed her into their midst and she knew she could rely on the coven. However, she was sadly lacking on the boyfriend front and she was mighty lonely coming home to an empty house. Well, not entirely empty, there was Snow, her big white cat.

"Okay, see you in a bit." Ella clicked the cell off and dropped it in her purse. She had two options; she could walk or ride Belle, her bike. She opted for Belle; her bike would be quicker than the twenty-minute walk to the other end of town.

Early on Sunday morning, the streets of Waxing were quiet. She pedaled down the tree-lined road breathing ocean air and enjoying the warmth of sunshine on her face. As she approached the fish vendors and docks, she noticed a boat moored out in the cove close to Turtle Point. Someone was standing on the bow unhooking a line from a buoy. She stopped and leaned her bike against the railing. She walked along the floating dock till she came to Oscar's slip, his boat should be there, only the *Red Moon* was gone.

She shaded her eyes against the intense morning sun. Past the jetty and Turtle Point, a red and white fishing boat lumbered over the water. The *Red Moon,* Oscar's boat. She sighed, too late. She'd check back after she got off work. Oscar usually didn't work on Sundays, he must be going to visit his family up the coast; maybe he'd be back early from wherever he was off to. She hoped he would return before sunset because she needed her truck fixed. The thought niggled at her perhaps he was fishing. She hoped not after the town meeting last night.

Back on Belle, she continued to the Crystal Witch gift shop and the breakfast which would be waiting for her.

After the short ride from the docks, Ella sat at the table in Hettie's small kitchen which served as break-room for the gift shop. She admired soft-boiled eggs sitting on a bed of toast and asparagus, resting on the plate in front of her. She picked up her fork. Hettie had whipped up blueberry-laden pancakes and sausage for a side. "Wow, what a spread. Fantastic!" Ella said between bites of syrupy pancake. "I truly do think you should open a café. You're such a good cook, Hettie."

"Aw, thanks." Hettie poured steaming coffee into a mug and placed it by Ella's plate. "Evan will be down soon. So I want to ask you something before he gets here." Hettie set the pot on the stove.

"Oh yeah, the girl to girl talk?"

"Yes. I...we...Evan asked me to marry him." Hettie didn't look happy at the prospect.

Ella set her fork down. "Is there a problem?"

"I came from the past—sixteen ninety-two, to be exact. What if Declan comes again? What if we can't stop him next time? And I end up traveling back to the past?"

Ella hastened around the table and embraced Hettie. "It was a good spell, a binding spell. He can't come back from the past." She pulled back and looked into Hettie's eyes as they overflowed with tears. "Darla is our High Priestess of the Coastal Coven, she worked and reworked the spell. You took the basic bones of the enchantment and added all necessary ingredients to make irrevocable Magick. Don't have doubts now, Hettie. You *can't* have doubts now. Belief is part of the spell!"

Hettie pulled away, grabbed a napkin, and dabbed at her eyes. "I know, I know. Don't understand why I'm so emotional."

"You said yes to Evan, didn't you?"

"I did."

"It's been eight months since Declan came through the curtain and tried to take you back. True, he is a warlock, an awful, terrible warlock. But you need to put Declan behind you." Ella clapped her hands. "You're getting married! We've got to celebrate. When? Where? I want details!"

"We haven't set a date. I wasn't sure if I should get married, but I feel I really need to, because of the...baby." The tentative smile on Hettie's face set Ella's heart racing.

Ella was breathless. "A baby! Wonderful, first new little witch in our coven, you are full of surprises today. I can't wait to tell the girls—well, your baby is your surprise to tell. What an absolutely wonderful day!"

The tread on the stair creaked, drawing attention to Evan, who stood in the doorway, a silly grin pasted on his face. "I'm stoked, best day ever. We're getting married." He spread his arms wide. "I vote for July. In fact I'm thinking the Fourth of July, a celebration like no other." His brow wrinkled. "Hettie wants to wait till after the baby is born."

He pulled a chair up and sat down. Hettie scooped asparagus, toast and soft boiled egg onto his plate. He smiled up at her. "Thanks, love."

Ella squealed with joy. "No, you should marry on the next full moon to ensure prosperity and happiness." She walked to the wall calendar and lifted the page. "This is May, h-m-m, June full moon is on a Wednesday, July, perfect, a full moon on July fourth!!" She could hardly believe the happy news, a wedding, a baby—such joy. There would be parties to plan, a baby shower, a bridal shower and a girl's night out. "When are you telling everyone?"

Hettie glanced at Evan, her eyes sparkled. "I guess soon. Our next coven meeting is Thursday. We should have a date set for sure by the gathering. Right, Evan?"

He picked up the paper napkin, wiped his face and put it on his empty plate. "The sooner the better far as I'm concerned. Well, ladies, I hate to leave you two, but I've a meeting at Noah's boat, concerning a job."

"Wait," Hettie said. "I'll fix a plate for Noah. You know how he loves sausage and pancakes."

"Did you get laid off from the trucking company?" Ella asked.

"No, I was only a temporary employee till Mr. Tuttle recovered from his back injury," he said. "I'd stay on but the company only needs one driver for the Waxing route." He took the cellophane-wrapped plate from Hettie. He reached his other arm out and pulled her close and kissed her full on the lips. "Later, love."

Ella emitted a heavy sigh; if only she could find someone like Evan, someone who would love her in spite of her Magical powers, in spite of her obsessive and exhaustive pursuit of scientific truth. "So what job is Evan applying for?"

Hettie sat down in her chair, lifted her mug of coffee, and took a sip. "Noah needs a deckhand. I'm not happy Evan's interested in the job, but I know he has dreamed of working on a boat full time, being on the sea. And there aren't a whole lot of job opportunities here in Waxing." She set her cup down. "Tell me what's going on in the lab, you know, your experiments? Any results at all?"

"Not yet. First round of tests were inconclusive. There was a slight amplification of the sample in one flask suggesting growth, minuscule growth." Ella drummed her fingers in a staccato rhythm on the table. "Poseidon wants an answer soon. You know how impatient he can be." The trident tattoo on her right shin began throbbing as if he knew they spoke of him. "Speak of the underwater king, he's calling me now."

"Did you see him last night?"

"No, I only spoke to James. He is going to investigate a bit for me out around Razor Island." Ella rubbed her shin. She pulled up her long skirt and looked at the tattoo. Not only throbbing, but a vivid red color, which meant she was to come immediately. "I considered asking Mischell to scout around and see what she could find out. Being a mermaid she is more in tune to the Magical side of the ocean than James, but I'm going to wait, see what James can discover."

"Has Mischell reached adulthood?"

"No! She's barely a teenager." Ella smiled. The pink haired mermaid-sprog held a special place in her heart. Ella had spent hours comforting Mischell when she had been banished from Atlantis into the care of three mermaids living off Waxing's shore.

# # #

Noah woke one shoe short of a pair. "What the hell?" He muttered. He searched everywhere, but couldn't find it. Finally giving up the search, he took off his remaining shoe and threw the canvas shoe through the open cabin door. Those were brand new Nikes; what did he do with his other one? He grabbed his deck boots from the storage container and jerked them on.

He untied the line from the buoy and cruised back to the marina and his slip. He put out fenders, tied the boat's lines and cut the engine. Rocking from the boat added to his pounding headache.

"Hey, Noah," Evan said. Half Native American, Evan Wolf represented his heritage well, keeping his jet-black hair long and sporting moccasin boots. "Brought you some of Hettie's special sausage and pancakes you like." He handed the plate off to Noah.

"Thanks, man." The food looked good, but his stomach began to roil. He had drunk the whole bottle of whiskey and now he'd pay the price. What the hell—he'd only been going to toast Bruce, one toast to his mate. Noah set the plate on the galley counter. He could heat the sausage and pancakes up for lunch after he got over his tidal wave of nausea. Not stopping after one toast to Bruce, or two. Poor decision that. Noah held out his hand. "Come on aboard. Good to see you, Evan."

"Like wise." Evan shook Noah's hand. "Oscar said you might need a deckhand. I worked the fishing fleet here during time off from high school, and the Marines." His grin was wide and infectious, and Noah found himself grinning back.

"Are you willing to work long hours sometimes for little pay?" He had always liked Evan; he was a reliable friend although Noah hadn't seen much of Evan the past four years. "When were you discharged?"

"Finished my tour ten months ago," he said. "My temp job for the delivery service is over and I'm looking for work." He shrugged. "I've always loved the ocean. I swear salt water runs through my veins." Evan sat down on the bench and looked out toward the morning sea, calm and dappled in pink. "Hettie and I are getting married."

"Congratulations." Noah thumped Evan on the back. "Man, you are one lucky dude. Hettie's a stand-up lady and beautiful."

"Watch it."

"Happy for you, man." Noah offered a fist bump.

"Thanks."

The hum of a vibrating cell had Evan digging in his pocket. "Hey, love, what's up?"

Evan's phone call gave Noah a chance to go into the galley to grab some aspirin and a mug of coffee. He poured a second cup for Evan. Back on deck, Evan said goodbye, closed his cell and took the offered cup.

"That call was from Hettie. Seems her friend is having a barbeque tonight to celebrate our engagement. You're invited; seven o'clock at Shell Cottage. You'll come, right?"

"I wouldn't miss a party!" Noah chuckled at Evan's enthusiasm. "Oh, and you've got the job if you want it. Now you'll have Hettie to consider, the pay isn't always great. Show up Monday. We'll take the Mystic Mermaid out so we can get a feel for her."

Evan stepped off the boat and turned. "Thanks for giving me a chance." Walking backward, he saluted. "See you tonight."

Noah went into the galley and grabbed two more aspirin, swallowing them with the last of his cold coffee. He lay down on his bunk, arm across his eyes. Maybe some shut-eye, and his headache would ease up. His mind drifted to the light-haired sea nymph he observed last night. Was she a hallucination? Could be, in the state he had been in. He didn't use to believe in sea nymphs, mermaids or any of those legends.

Not until the accident left him drifting in the ocean for three days and took Bruce's life. Not until a pink haired nymph or mermaid had told him everything would be all right. Not until she had helped him onto the raft, saving him from certain drowning.

#

Six cottages stood on Turtle Lane all were baptized with beach-themed names. Noah was thankful the five-minute walk from the dock had cleared all the cobwebs from his mind. He continued walking to the end of the lane, where Shell Cottage sat. Hinges creaked as he pushed open the white picket gate. The cottage was encased in weathered gray wood siding, and white trim was the icing on the house. Flower boxes filled with red geraniums hung under the windows. Laughter drifted from around back.

He couldn't remember who lived here since old Mr. Jensen had died. He followed along a slate path which wove past the side of the cottage through a manicured rose garden and emptied out on to a cement slab. Close to a dozen locals stood around a crackling fire pit.

Recognition sparked as his eyes met hers—the crazy chick from the gift shop. Whatever she called herself, scientist, and environmentalist, whatever; now he remembered, *she* lived here. The big metal building out back was her lab. And she was headed his way. He should leave. Tonight was Evan and Hettie's night. He didn't want to spoil their party. He turned on his heel and headed back toward rose garden.

"Wait! Mr. Drago, please." Something in her voice stopped him.

He turned around. "I shouldn't have come. I didn't realize you lived here."

She placed her hand on his sleeve. "Hmmm, can we put aside our differences for tonight? For Hettie and Evan's party?"

The sea breeze left a chill in the air, but where she touched, his arm burned like a hot summer day. She bit her lip, a pleading look on her face.

He stared for a moment, not sure if he was annoyed or glad. "Sure." A catch in his throat had him coughing.

She grabbed his hand and pulled him back to the party. "Look what I found lurking in the rose bed—Mr. Drago."

She had done something fascinating to her white blonde hair piled high on her head, a string of pink shells woven in and out. "Noah. Call me Noah. Mr. Drago is my father." He stopped, turning her to face him. "And you are?"

"Ella Stone. Welcome to 'Shell Cottage.'" She smiled coolly, gauging him, sea green eyes sparkling like emeralds.

"Thanks." He withdrew his hand. She swayed as she walked away, leaving his imagination to decide what lie beneath her long flowing pale blue dress

"Noah, over here," Evan waved at him from the horseshoe pits.

# # #

Ella was surprised to see the brooding boat captain show up at the gathering. She'd make the most of his presence. Maybe get to know him better. When she'd faced him and met his eyes, there was a connection. He was all turbulent sea inside, resistant to human contact—because of the boat accident or his mate drowning and disappearing? She would find out. Maybe mend the fence with him; she realized she'd spoke out of line at the Crystal Witch shop. His soul needed healing. She could help him with that. Something pulled her toward him; before she knew it, she stood next to him by the horseshoe pits.

Noah laughed a deep throaty sound that reverberated through her. He smelled of wind and sea. He turned to look at her, his shadow of a beard giving him a mysterious, wicked look.

"Would one of you gentlemen help me get my barbeque fired up?" she asked.

Noah glanced at Evan. "Actually we're…" He gestured toward the horseshoe pit.

"Go ahead, Noah, I'll call you when we've finished playing." Evan threw his horseshoe, striking the pole with a loud clank.

Witch's intuition, she supposed; he was troubled, didn't like conflict and felt he'd get it from her. She tried to ignore her sense something would change tonight; something was in the air.

Chapter Three

After the small party of friends had played games, eaten and toasted the engaged couple, most of them had drifted on home. Evan, Hettie, Noah and Ella were the only ones left. They sat around warm fire pit the coals still glowing. Noah placed a couple more logs on the coals sending sparks dancing in the air. The wood caught and flames blazed to life. Ella felt lightheaded; she had probably had one too many glasses of wine, she closed her eyes briefly. Open again, she glanced sideways and her eyes met Noah's. Why was she drawn to him?

"Funny thing happened last night," Noah said. Clearing his throat, he continued, "I drank too much, fell asleep on my boat, or passed out or both. When I woke up, one of my new Nike tennis shoes was gone."

Hettie giggled. "Are you sure you didn't throw your shoe overboard during your inebriated state?"

Evan laughed and Noah joined in.

Heat crept up Ella's face. Was James stealing again? Her familiar had a fetish for collecting sandals, shoes and boots, basically anything worn on a human foot. "It'll probably turn up," she said with a confidence she really didn't feel.

Evan stood and offered Hettie his hand.

Hettie grasped Evan's hand and stood up. "I think we better head home. Thanks for the wonderful party, Ella. You are such a treasure, and I'm lucky to call you my friend."

Evan stood and hooked an arm around his bride-to-be. "This has been the best day of my life." He pulled Hettie close, kissing the top of her head. "I get my dream job thanks to you, Noah, and this wonderful engagement party. Thanks, Ella."

Noah stuffed his hands in his pockets. "See you on the dock bright and early. We're taking the boat out."

"I'll be there." Evan waved, grabbed Hettie's hand and they left.

The fire kept the darkness at bay. He hadn't meant to stay so long, and certainly hadn't meant to be the last one to leave.

"Would you care for a cup of coffee before you go?" She found she'd enjoyed his company and didn't want him to leave.

"No thanks. I walked over. I'm sleeping on my boat tonight." He took a step back, getting ready to make his escape.

"Everyone has left but us." She told him in a soothing melodious tone. "I'd really like to tell you my side of the discussion on closing the fleets' fishing grounds for two weeks."

His eyes narrowed. "Hey, party was great. You're a nice lady. Let's leave it at that."

"Would you come back tomorrow, please?"

"Why?"

From his tone she could tell he didn't quite trust her intentions.

She brushed a loose strand of hair behind her ear. "I want to share what I've discovered in my lab, if you're interested?"

"Are you hitting on me?" He rubbed the back of his neck, not making eye contact.

Poor man, he was definitely in need of healing.

"Not hitting on you, more like trying to open your eyes."

He shrugged. "Sure, why not? What time?"

"I'll be done running tests by six o'clock. How'd seven be?"

He took another step back and lifted his hand in a halfhearted wave. "Seven sounds good."

Magick stirred inside of her; she lifted a hand to his retreating back. "Sleep well, captain," she murmured. Magick left her fingertips, swirling around him, stopping him. He glanced over his shoulder before leaving.

Ella sat watching as the fire slowly died. Snow purred and rubbed against her legs. She reached down and scratched the insistent cat. "Some party, huh, Snow? I like the captain. He's quite blustery on the outside but tender on the inside. He's been hurt, you know—the loss of his friend and his boat."

A coyote howled close by and Snow jumped into Ella's lap.

"That coyote won't bother you here." She stroked the cat. Snow hissed and dug her claws into Ella's shoulder through her woolen sweater. She set Snow down and watched the big white cat run toward the laboratory. A dark shadow slid around the corner of the building and disappeared in the dark woods.

"Snow! Come back." Her heart raced. "Here kitty, kitty." Snow came back around the corner and complained all the way back to Ella. "What did you see out there?" She held Snow close, petting her. "You are too small to fend off a coyote. Let's get you inside. How does a saucer of milk sound?"

Snow purred her agreement and kneaded Ella's sweater.

Once inside, Ella set Snow down on the soft cushion on the rocking chair. While milk warmed on the stove for herself, she poured a saucer of milk for Snow. She sat down at the desk and opened her journal. A loud metallic crash sounded outside. She jumped up and flipped on the porch light. She peeked out the window to discover a piece of old rusted corrugated tin rested against her Toyota. And yet there was no wind or breeze or even a slight draft which could account for the force which threw the tin against her truck.

From her vantage point at the window, she could see the decorative windmill in her yard standing still, not a breath of air moved. Howling much closer now, definitely not a coyote sent cold fingers of fear dancing up her spine. The keening was otherworldly and close. Snow arched her back, hair standing on end and hissed her displeasure.

Ella slid the deadbolt in place on the back door and secured it. Her heart raced. She ran for the front door. After securing the front, she raced to every window, locking and pulling shades down.

She stood in the middle of the living room panting, hands over her ears to block out the howling. Finally, she removed her hands and listened. Silence. She mumbled a protection spell for her house. Nothing could cross into *her space* now unless invited.

What should she do? Call Darla, the High Witch? Contact Poseidon? Something bad had come to town, she knew deep in her soul. But what would she say, there's howling and things are blowing around my yard? No, better wait till she had more proof something evil was in the wind.

Her cell rang startling her. She took a deep breath to ease tightness gathered in her chest and picked the cell up. "Hello?" She sounded shakier than she would have liked.

"Ella? What's wrong?" Hettie sounded confused.

"Nothing…something…I don't know what to do."

"What's going on?"

"When I got home, there was a keening sound outside. There's evil come to our town. Why I don't know. I feel like I'm being singled out. A clear sky, no wind and a four-by-six piece of corrugated tin slammed into my truck tonight." Ella took a deep breath trying to calm her nerves. "Snow went out and I saw a shadow turn the corner of the lab and disappear, followed by a bone-chilling keening."

"Oh, honey, maybe a rogue gust of wind; you know how we get those here on the coast. And the keening? Probably a coyote," Hettie said, confidently.

"I hope you're right." Maybe she had jumped to the wrong conclusion. "The sound, the keening, didn't sound like a coyote. I'm tired—maybe my imagination was working overtime." She paced to the window and peeked out. All appeared calm in her moonlit backyard.

"Do you want me to come over?"

"No, no. I placed a protection spell on my house. I should be all right till morning." She fingered the mermaid locket she always wore.

"I was calling to thank you again for the wonderful party. I'll stop by tomorrow before work. Goodnight."

"Goodnight." Ella ended the call and plugged her cell into the power source. She made a cup of calming tea in her favorite flowered cup. She sat rocking in her chair, took a sip of tea and set her cup on the end table. Kitty jumped in her lap and settled down for the night. Around four in the morning, Ella finally drifted to sleep.

She didn't hear the windows rattling or the scratching at the doors.

# # #

The waves crashed on Turtle Point, the air vibrated with a dull roar. Annoying, Noah thought, how easily he agreed to meet her tomorrow evening. He'd meant to say no. The excuse he needed never surfaced. Damn annoying. He would have come off like a jerk without a damn good excuse. Well, they would meet tomorrow night at seven. She would try to convince him she was right, he'd not agree, they'd argue and that would be the end of the discussion.

Ella was making the effort, so he supposed he should too. Maybe he should bring a peace offering? Candy? No, too personal. wine? Yes, he'd bring wine.

He reached the *Mystic Mermaid,* saw Oscar's light on and rapped on *Red Moon's* deck.

"Ahoy, Oscar?"

The old man grumbled like a bear trying to open a honey pot, finally swinging the cabin door open, and emerging into the night air. "What's up? Better be good, get an old man out of his bunk." He swung a beam of light toward Noah. "Hey, young fella, what's going on?"

"Wanted to let you know I hired Evan, and thank you for the recommendation."

"Good, good. You goin' out in the morning?" Oscar patted his nightshirt pocket, pulling out a cigar stub.

"Trial run to see how the boat handles, and how Evan does. We'll probably fish later in the week. I'm expecting my permit in the mail soon." Not wanting to turn in quite yet, he flipped on the *Mystic Mermaid's* outside light. "You want a beer or coffee?"

The moon had risen and bathed the grizzled old man in a white light. "I'll sit a spell if you don't mind. No drinks for me. Can't be getting up all night using the head; won't be any good for fishin' tomorrow."

Noah chuckled. "I hear you. Well, come over and sit a spell." He set up two deck chairs.

Long after Oscar had returned to his boat, Noah sat gazing at the ocean and in particular Turtle Point. No lady of the sea showed herself tonight. He sighed, folded up the chairs and went below to bed.

Next morning pounding on the cabin door jolted him out of a deep sleep. Last thing he remembered from last night was pulling his blanket up under his chin. He'd slept all night. For the first time since the accident, *he'd slept all night long.*

Rising sun poured through the porthole, hitting him square in the face. He jumped out of bed and opened the door. Evan stood there a silly grin plastered on his face, holding two cups of steaming coffee.

Chapter Four

Ella ran crashing through the woods. Howling laced with a fierce anger was right behind her. She tried to outrun the pounding footsteps, but the footfalls were getting closer and closer. Heat of an evil breath scorched her neck. Far away in the distance, Hettie shouted her name.

Ella woke with a start and lay gasping for breath. Hettie pounded on the door. "Ella! Are you in there? Please open the door!"

"I'm coming, Hettie." She pulled the quilt around her shoulders against the chill in the morning air and padded barefoot to the front door. Ella held her palm out toward the door, releasing the spell; bolts slid and locks clicked open, and the door swung inward. "Come in, come in." She waved Hettie in and closed the door, locked it again.

"What took you so long to answer the door?" Panic laced Hettie's voice.

"I didn't sleep well last night." She stifled a yawn. "I had an awful nightmare. Whatever was wailing last night was chasing me through the woods. I remember passing the hemlock tree, near our coven's sacred circle. Evil is what I sensed. I never saw anything, but I know something is coming or is already here in Waxing." She tossed the quilt on the couch and grabbed an oversized wool sweater from the back of the kitchen chair.

"My dream was weird. I haven't been that frightened since I exposed Kenn's scheme to overthrow Poseidon and claim the throne." Hairs prickled on the back of her neck. "You know Kenn tried to kill me once. Poseidon banished him from the royal city of Atlantis. Not for trying to kill me, but for stealing Poseidon's sandals."

"Just a dream," Hettie said, hugging her.

"Yes, but dream or no, it seemed so real." Her dream and the headache that followed pushed down on her spirit. "I might not be able to figure out what's causing the die-off before time runs out. The answer is eluding me and that is troubling."

"Your concern would explain the helplessness you felt in your dream. Your subconscious made up a scenario to deal with your stress." Hettie took a seat at the small, drop-leaf oak table in the kitchen. "When do you meet Poseidon?"

"Tonight, James will let me know when His Majesty has arrived." She busied herself making tea for both of them, still not quite buying Hettie's explanation of her dream. "And there is also another matter, that of the captain."

"The captain?" Hettie frowned.

"Noah. He is in such a world of hurt from his accident, losing his boat, and more importantly, his friend." She set two cups of steaming tea on the table. "Our beliefs are not the same on what is going on, although he's coming by tonight to talk. He'll hear my side of the situation." Ella took a sip of tea, setting her seagrass colored cup down with a clink on the matching saucer. "He needs closure, the death of his friend, the loss of his boat."

Hettie sat straighter. "You've always had a thing for strays. Now, a good looking sea captain whose heart is hurting has got to be *irresistible* to you."

"I want to help." Did she want to help? Or did she see something more in the captain, a need, something she could fulfill? "Would you like me to open the Crystal Witch this morning, or could I take a nap first?"

"Why don't you come in around noon? I really appreciate you subbing for me. I know Monday isn't your regular day, and I wouldn't ask except my doctor appointment has been changed. It's this afternoon now."

"No problem. I'm moving kind of slow today, noon will work fine." She stifled a yawn. "Plus, my experiments won't be done till around five, so no need to hurry." She'd still have time to change clothes and run a brush through her hair before Noah showed up later today.

"Evan said he and Noah should return approximately one o'clock. Evan's taking me on an evening picnic the radio said sunset is at seven forty-five. I'll have enough time to fix a picnic basket up if you wouldn't mind closing tonight?" Hettie blushed and her ebony eyes sparkled.

"Sure, I don't mind. I'm meeting Noah here at seven, and if I close by five I'll have time to check lab results before he arrives."

The gift shop had a busy day. Ella did not sit down from the time she arrived until she left at five o'clock. She put her bag of candles in Belle's basket and pedaled toward home. Pushing her bike through the front gate she headed to the backyard. With her senses heightened; she could tell someone was behind her house, in the back yard. Rounding the corner of the house, she let out a sigh of relief, when a grizzled Oscar emerged from under the hood of her truck.

"Oscar I'm glad to see you." She threw her arms around him in a genuine hug of happiness. "I didn't see your truck? What's the prognosis?"

He straightened, took his stub of a cigar out of his mouth and put it in his pocket. "I walked over from the dock. Looks like the battery life is gone, used up. I cleaned up the spark plugs. They seem to be okay." He slammed the hood down. "I'll bring my charger by. We'll see if we can get this vehicle goin'. Take her down to Jake's Auto and he'll put a new battery in for you." He took a red kerchief out of his pants pocket and wiped his hands on it.

"What do I owe you?" Ella laid her hand on his arm.

"Not a damn thing, girl."

"I can whip something up for dinner tomorrow night?" Oscar was a crotchety widower and didn't get many home-cooked meals. She was betting he'd take a homemade dinner in payment.

He stuck his stogie back in his mouth, worked it for a few seconds before answering. "Now you mention dinner, I wouldn't mind some of your home-cooked chili and cornbread." Oscar rolled his eyes skyward, he seemed to be deciding if he dare say more. "Would be obliged for a pot of chili; might last me a few days, maybe even a week."

Ella squeezed his arm. "You bet." She'd throw in a spell for health for the old guy. Make extra special chili.

"All right, then." He waved. "Be back later, I'll bring my charger." His boots crunched on gravel as he made his way to the front of the house.

"Bye, Oscar, and thanks."

She tidied up the living area in her house which didn't take long. The living room was cluttered, but it would do. With a flick of her wrist, new candles in old fashioned glass holders burst to life. Her house was muddled but clean. The piles of *Scientific Journals* and *Science Digests* were piled high in neat stately mounds on her dining room table. Other magazines were in neat stacks on the floor along the wall.

On her cherry wood desk sat a computer, weather monitoring station and a pile of printouts from *The Oceanography Society*. Well, she wasn't spending any more time cleaning. After all, this wasn't a social call Noah was making. She might not mind a social call, considering his handsome face and his physique. Heat flushed her cheeks and she picked up a magazine and fanned herself.

Enough said! They'd head to the lab as soon as Noah arrived. She busied herself in the small kitchen. Washed and dried the few grimy dishes she had used earlier. Put the dishes away in the cupboards, wiped down the stove, and counters. Started coffee and took two mugs down. Would he even want coffee?

In half an hour at seven Noah would be here. She threw a lab coat on and headed across the backyard to her lab. Best get the lab organized, she thought, before he arrived. Once inside, the lab came alive. Things were happening, humming, creaking; she loved being in here. She went to the locker where she kept her gloves and goggles, put them on. Walking around the steel worktables, she stopped to adjust a temperature on a Bunsen burner.

Humming and buzzing of the aquarium's filtration equipment drew her toward her pet projects. Sea anemones and other native cold water invertebrates had attached to the small, sculpted shipwreck in the first of three two-thousand gallon saltwater aquariums lining the back wall of the lab.

Three half grown green fish, Coris Warasse, swam by. She hadn't put too many fish in the tank because she was concentrating on the invertebrates. Dahlia anemones, their red columns sporting grey verrucae and white tentacles swayed gently back and forth in the current from the filtration system.

She pressed her palm against the side, and delighted in the vibration from the underwater world, as life teemed beyond the glass barrier.

The thrill of receiving a grant last month to work on rebuilding reefs left her breathless. Rebuilding reefs had started all over the world, and now she was a part of the process. Massachusetts had approved artificial reef guidelines in 2008. Outside of material properties and surface area recommendations, the guidelines were wide open for how such structures should be shaped. She was using artwork similar to Jason de Caries Taylor's underwater museum in Cancun. Only instead of human-looking statues for invertebrates to attach to, she was collaborating with local artists here in Waxing. Finding specialized materials the critters would attach to and colonize was the first part of the process.

Their successful populations would clean sea water naturally and draw greater numbers of fish and shellfish to the area, she mused.

She walked over to the next aquarium. This artist had created a giant liberty bell, a crack from the bottom to half way up. Enough room for small schools of hatchlings to hide from predators. Reef systems full of life would be another tourist attraction to bring people to Waxing during summer time. Scuba divers could visit a living, learning underwater art museum. If she had any luck, she would convert more people to her cause of preserving the ocean.

Finally, she took a sample of death-gunk, RTB-1, from the petri dish and put it on a slide. Once she had focused the microscope over the slide, she watched in disbelief. Terror flooded her body. She observed the sample increasing in size at an astronomical rate. This was a big change, a bad change from the slow growth of yesterday.

A car door slammed, and she hurried to let Noah in. Punctual; she liked that.

He carried a tall, thin paper bag. Wine? "Good evening, Noah."

He pulled a bottle out of the sack and held the wine out to her. 'Plantation Red' from Mill River Winery, one of her favorite wines. He arched an eyebrow. "Peace offering. I think we got off on the wrong foot at the store the other day."

She accepted his gift running her fingers over the white label, a drawing of a red-winged blackbird sitting on a cattail. She cradled the bottle in her arm. "Thanks." She wavered, even wine wouldn't lift her mood right now.

"Something happen?" His eyebrows raised in question. "Ella?" He took her other arm and ushered her into the lab, closed the door.

"I...the specimen grew at a rate I've never seen before." Leading the way over to two microscopes positioned side by side, she indicated he should look through each of them. His closeness sent a shiver dancing up her spine. "The scope on the left is the sample from yesterday. A new specimen is on the slide on the right scope. Overnight growth is astounding. Do you see the difference?" Her breath caught in her throat as her heart pounded in her chest. She shifted the bottle she still held.

"I see, amazing," he said, wonder filling his voice. He studied each specimen for a few more seconds before flashing his chocolate brown eyes at her.

Suddenly she was aware of him, so very aware of every inch of him. She looked away first, carefully setting the wine bottle on the lab table. "The organism is killing the flora and fauna. The die-off started out past Razor Island, at around ninety feet deep."

She picked up a notebook and wrote down her findings for today. She wished he'd quit staring. Nervous, she tapped her pen against her notebook. "Think what happens with an algae bloom, we have a similar problem. When blooms run out of steam the bacteria move in and feed on the dying algae literally sucking the oxygen out of the water in the process and creating a dead zone."

He shifted and hooked his thumbs in his jean pockets. She had his attention now; he was definitely interested in what she had to say. "Unlike algae and bacteria responsible for blooms, which may be toxic or not, this organism is aggressive and feeding off flora and fauna, killing all sea life it comes in contact with and multiplying like crazy." She sighed, closed her notebook.

"There aren't any signs that the organism is slowing down. I have noticed there are indications the bacterium are closer to the surface now, on kelp leaves. A dead zone wouldn't do the fisheries or town any good."

She spread her hands wide, palms up. "Do you see what we are up against? I have to find the source, the cause and put an end to this Razor Toxic Bloom. Before it reaches Waxing."

"How do you plan to find the…source?" He frowned, eyes even under drawn brows. "Shouldn't you report this matter to the Massachusetts Department of Fish and Game?"

She hated the thought of lying to him but the truth would be harder for him to swallow. "With part of my grant money I received I purchased more up to date equipment, most of the equipment is still on backorder. The rest is to apply to any research done off the Atlantic coast." She smiled. "If I feel it necessary, I'll inform the government, but right now there's the very real possibility I can take care of said problem and keep it local."

She took off her lab coat and goggles and hung them on the wooden coatrack next to the door.

"I have a few leads I'm checking out." She didn't believe bringing up Poseidon to Noah was a good idea. "Come let's have a glass of wine. We'll talk, and I've printed out some scientific papers which may shed light on the situation for you."

"I assumed science was dry, but after looking through your scope at those tiny convicts, well, it was mind-blowing."

"To me, science is the essence of discovery, finding the right pieces to solve the puzzle. The possibilities are endless. I'm a scientist and I strive for perfection in my results." Her teeth worried her bottom lip. Old habit, she thought. A moment later she caught his gaze riveted on said lip, and she headed for the door.

He grabbed the bottle of red wine off the pristine metal lab table and followed her out the door.

# # #

Darkness had edged in, Ella flipped on lights as she walked through the cottage. After she handed him a corkscrew, she set two crystal wine glasses on the carved rosewood coffee table situated between them.

Noah decided he had made a dangerous mistake coming here. Dangerous because he wanted to believe her; he found he wanted to get to know Ella better. When she worried her bottom lip with her teeth, he couldn't stop staring. What would her lips feel like pressed against his?

She handed him a sheaf of papers. "Start reading these. Top one talks about climate change and the effects on phytoplankton, which might have something to do with the unknown growth in the pelagic and photic zones."

He looked up from the paper and transfixed on her sea green eyes. "Yeah, sure. I'll read them over." Maybe he could take these papers home and sit, his dictionary beside him, and figure it out. Crap! Pelagic zone, what the hell?

"Any questions? I'll be happy to explain." She smiled.

"Do you mind if I take these papers home?"

"No. I made copies for myself." She went to her desk and brought a manila envelope for him to stash papers in. One paper she held close to her chest. "This, Captain, is my conclusions so far. Please don't show my results to anyone else."

"You have my word." He held out his hand, amazed she would trust him, her findings were important. He was still curious why she wasn't reporting any of her findings to the EPA or NOAA or somewhere. Was she trying to earn a Noble Prize in one of the sciences for her work? What if she failed to stop the bacterium, and waited too long to involve government agencies?

He was intrigued by her. Enthusiasm for her work carried over into her eyes. Eyes a warm sea green set far enough apart in her heart-shaped face. When she slipped off her shoes, sat on the blue couch, and tucked her slender legs under her she reminded him of a mermaid. Slender and graceful; he wasn't attracted to her, was he? Who was he fooling—of course he was.

They talked for an hour and polished off the bottle of wine. Noah gathered up the documents, his homework. "I better go, got an early day tomorrow."

Ella took the bottle and glasses to the kitchen.

"Well, thanks for coming over," she said in a silky tone. She opened the back door. He stepped out, she followed close behind.

Night air infused by an early spring chill met them as they moved on to the tiny back porch and into moon light.

"I'm glad we got together tonight." He said and found he meant it. "Let me know when you're free sometime and I'll take you out for a boat ride."

"Sounds lovely," she moved in closer to him.

He wanted nothing more than to kiss her. Her eyes sparkled with reflected moonlight, a fleeting look of yearning passed over her face. He reached out grasped her shoulders and pulled her close. Not a friendly kiss and not a deeply passionate kiss. A tentative, enjoyable kiss, long enough to take his breath away and leave him wanting more.

She sighed when he pulled away, a smile quivered over her lips.

She smelled of cinnamon and spice, sweet and fresh as his Mom's homemade snickerdoodle cookies. She trembled beneath his hands. Reluctantly he released her. "Goodnight, Ella."

"Goodnight, Noah," she whispered, before turning and going inside. The door closed and the lock clicked into place. He whistled a tune softly, all the way to his car.

Chapter Five

Ella touched her fingertips to her lips. He had kissed her. She hadn't resisted. She had been aware of every inch of him and his breath on her cheek while he kissed her. A pleasant surprise as the kiss was unexpected.

Lady Ella, James' deep rich baritone sounded in her head. *Poseidon has arrived. I'll meet you at the end of Turtle Point to escort you to see him.*

I'll meet you there, James. Give me half an hour. Are you still living in the same den?

Oh, yes. My home sweet home is quite lovely. I've a pathway completed to the entrance. I will show you tonight. Ciao.

Ciao.

Ella cast a protection spell on her cottage and lab. She prepared herself on her walk to the ocean. Her metamorphosis took a few minutes. By the time she reached Turtle Point, her gills were functioning. Her eyes and ears were protected from the salt water. The change was complete. She stripped down to the long gauzy slip she wore under her dress; her hair was loose and hung down her back. The moon was higher in the sky now, and cast light across the sandy beach.

She waded out and dove into the next wave. The thrill of swimming into the depths of the ocean unencumbered by the need of equipment to keep her alive was something she never got tired of. Twenty minutes later she arrived at Razor Island. She glided down to James' den located in the rock base of the island. James, an old soul octopus, emerged and lightly hugged her with four of his tentacles, while four other tentacles held him upright.

She was lucky to have James. Most octopuses only lived for two years. James had once been a mer-soldier for Poseidon. James lost Poseidon's favor, because of his shoe fetish. Unable to resist the God-of-the-Sea's favorite pair of gold and jewel encrusted sandals, James was brought before Poseidon for stealing, a serious crime in Atlantis.

Poseidon punished him by turning him into an octopus. Ella needed a trustworthy familiar and the rest is history. James would be free of his octopus form after ten more years. He would be a mer-man again and free to roam the seas.

Do you like my new entrance? He asked, pointing by means of one outstretched tentacle at a path lined with shoes, sandals and boots, all color coordinated.

Oh, James, I thought you weren't going to steal anymore!

Don't sound so disappointed. I quit stealing, well, except for this one. He wrapped his tentacle around a Nike tennis shoe and lifted it for Ella to see.

Her eyes widened. This tennis shoe belonged to, Noah! James seemed lost in his musings. He pointed out new additions to his shoe collection. *All the rest were lost by their owners, single ones, and found by me. I'm especially proud of this one, a Jimmy Choo.*

He lovingly caressed the smart looking hot pink high heel, the sole a signature red. *I was under a party boat, and what should fall over the side and into my tentacle but this beauty.*

The Nike belongs to a friend of mine. Do you suppose you could return the shoe? She had no idea why James focus was shoes.

For you darling, I will. Tonight, I promise. Come now, we don't want to keep his lordship waiting. You ready to ride? He wiggled his eyes up and down.

I'm ready!

James wrapped one long tentacle gently but firmly around her waist. She linked her arms around two of his. On a whoosh of water, he propelled them to Poseidon's waiting submersible.

One of her favorite things to do was ride along with James. Her hair streamed behind her and they virtually flew over the bottom. Starfish dotted rocks close to the island, seahorses darted in and out of kelp, and her favorite, sea ferns, swayed with the current. They dove to ninety feet where the desolation began, where the bottom was depleted and dying. The devastation brought a heaviness to her chest.

The ride ended too soon. James set her down in front of a silver gourd shaped marine craft. Triangular windows emitted a welcoming light. The windows adorned the length of the craft like jewels. She stepped through the door of the sea-pod, secured the door and swam up through glistening waters of the moon pool. She emerged into an air filled chamber, directly outside the door to Poseidon's throne room.

She walked to the dressing room across the hall. Inside she wrung out her hair and exchanged her wet clothes for the dry robe of luxurious cloth that had been left on a brass hook for her. Poseidon had his moments, and this was one of the nicer ones. She preferred speaking to telepathy and he obliged her by arriving in the submersible, which had air-locked compartments.

Ella knocked on his chamber door. A tall mer-guard opened the door and showed her in.

Poseidon reclined on blue silk and green satin pillows set inside an enormous clamshell. On top of his black dreadlocks sat a golden crown encrusted with sparkling gems. Naked from his waist up except for two gold bands around each massive forearm, he motioned Ella forward.

"Your lordship," Ella bowed down.

"Rise, sea witch," he boomed, the sound echoing in the small room. "What know ye of the devastation riddling my ocean?"

"I've come to the conclusion a bacterium has been introduced by someone who knows the sea well." She pulled the robe tighter.

"Hm-m, would you like to know what I think?" He stood up, posture stiff, muscles flexed.

"Of course, Your Majesty."

"This 'someone' is searching for treasure. Think about it, if the ocean is barren, wouldn't finding treasure be much easier?"

"The Golden Sea Horse would be the only treasure along the coast here. My mother told me the story many years ago."

He waved his hand dismissively. "No, no. There is much treasure here, buried on the bottom under the sand. More gold and gems than any one human could spend in a lifetime. I'd bet my last coinage our destroyer is also a thief. Treasure means nothing to me, but we have to protect the ocean."

"Any hypothesis if a human or Magical creature is responsible for the damage to the ocean?" She prayed he would have a clue to help her find the answer.

Poseidon sat down and leaned forward, elbows on his knees, his big head in his hands. "I don't know, sea witch. You need to find out, and soon. Time is running out. I will keep in contact through James. If I discover anything I'll let you know and you can do the same." He sat up.

Ella bowed. "I'll be in contact, Your Majesty."

"Sea Witch," he boomed, his eyes hooded. A wicked smile graced his face. "I have a claim on you." He shook his finger at her. "I granted your desire to build an underwater museum. If you can save the ocean without outside human help, you'll no longer owe me. We both know bringing human government agencies into your investigation would lead them to impose rules, regulations etc., etc., etc." He waved his hand in the air. "And *I want none of that!!*" His thunderous declaration was followed by his fist pounding the wooden arm of the clam chair.

He reclined back on the oversized pillows. "However, if you fail you will perpetually be mine. I've never had a sea witch in my bed, which I will right before I change you into—a mermaid. You won't be leaving the ocean ever. Your metamorphosis will be everlasting. I'm thinking a mermaid form might suit you fine. You've already got lovely green hair and those iridescent scales makes me hard looking at you."

Ella could feel the flush creeping up her neck and face. What a jerk! He thought to make her his concubine.

"We're working for the same thing, an ocean free of destruction, free of human interference." He sat, picked up his trident staff and touched it with reverence. "Do I make myself clear, Ella?"

"Crystal," Ella spit out.

The old goat! Ella knew a promise when she heard one. He had been trying for years to make her a member of his harem. She turned and ran out of the chamber, his booming laughter following her.

Back in the sea, she summoned James and they started back to shore. *Poseidon is an ass! He wants me permanently as one of his servants or lovers or both, if I can't fix this problem in the ocean.* Her chest tightened, and she hugged the tentacles close, comforted by the giant beast.

I've an idea, James ventured. *You said the devastation is caused by someone. What if one of his majesty's many mistresses is looking for revenge?*

But how would I find out?

I'll do a little research; see what I can discover.

James! Stop, look over there. There's a light in that trench.

Odd, first time I've seen a light there. Want to investigate?

I can't. Another time. You know my metamorphosis is on a timer right now, and I'll be changing back to human form soon.

Ella checked the underwater landmarks so she could find this exact location again. Her metamorphosis was not permanent, at least not yet. By the time she was back on shore, her hair was pale green and sparkling scales of iridescent aqua covered parts of her legs and arms. Gills on her neck had disappeared after she had emerged from the water; the changes back to human form depended on how long she'd been submerged.

Well after two a.m., she stood on the sandy shore of Turtle Point and gave thanks for a safe trip to Amphitrite, goddess of the sea and Poseidon's clueless wife. The wife Poseidon would betray if Ella were his mistress.

The trident tattoo had quit throbbing now their meeting was over. She lifted her long wet slip, the better to examine her legs. Scales flashed in the moonlight—such a pretty color—and started to disappear.

She looked up to see Noah, striding with purpose toward where she stood. Her heartbeat racing, nearly exploding, she couldn't let him discover her secret.

Slightly weak from her change, she gathered her Magick and sent him sprawling in the sand. Collecting the damp fabric of her slip in one hand, she mustered her strength and escaped up the grassy embankment.

Chapter Six

Noah didn't understand how he could sleep so well last night and tonight sleep eluded him like crazy. Didn't help he'd kissed Ella. He tossed and turned. He dreamed of kissing her again, of holding her tight, and craving her. Around two thirty a.m., he got up for the last time and made coffee. He pulled on his red and black mackinaw jacket and headed on deck. He sat down and inhaled his first sip of black gold and choked on the coffee. She was back. The sea nymph hadn't been the result of a Balvenie whiskey induced hallucination.

She stood in the moonlight, a dazzling sheen on her light colored hair. He leaped off the boat and ran the length of the dock. He'd find out who or what she was.

He rounded a rock outcropping on the beach. She was still there. Her pale hair fell like a curtain across her face when she leaned over to examine her leg. Her leg from where he stood looked shiny, sparkly as if covered in miniature sequins, and a second later her skin looked normal! Hair fanned across her face, fell away as she straightened up and spotted him, she pointed an outstretched hand toward him; a jolt sent him sprawling in the sand. *What the...*

He coughed, spit sand out of his mouth and stood up, brushing sand from his eyes. When at last he could see again the mysterious woman with pale-Blonde hair, and a long graceful gown had disappeared. It was a struggle to climb up the sandy embankment, but he made it. He searched the moonlit sands and the road paralleling the bay she wasn't anywhere. Rumble from crashing waves seemed to jeer at him.

Finally, he spotted her. A whisper of white weaving between the forest trees had him sprinting toward the woods across the road. Once in the forest he slowed, low hanging branches scratched his arms and face. Sweating, he discarded his jacket. Close now to the vision in white, he was guided by moonlight sifting through towering trees. A minute, no more he'd catch up with her.

When he lost sight of her, his heart beat like a drum in his chest. He rounded a tree. Out of breath, he leaned against a sturdy trunk. Blinking sweat from his eyes revealed he was on the edge of a clearing. She kneeled before an ancient hemlock tree, a tree he remembered the environmentalists had saved five years ago. Her palms pressed against the bark on the trunk. She spoke in a language he didn't recognize. A buzzing filled his head. He was drawn into the clearing. Stepping into open space ringed by forest, he wanted with every fiber of his being to call out to her, but he didn't want to scare her away.

When she turned her head and noticed him, she froze.

He had found his sea nymph. High above now, the moon shone down on the clearing like a spotlight. She stood up and turned to him. He could barely make out the hint of light green in her hair now, and her arms had a pale dusting of iridescent pale-green scales. Seaweed laced through her hair. His heart skipped a beat. Those sweet lips he had kissed hours earlier. He wasn't hallucinating.

This was Ella.

Ella backed away in quick, jerky steps. Fright filled her eyes.

"Ella." Noah held out his hand. "Let me take you back to Shell Cottage." He didn't know what was going on, but he intended to find out.

She pointed her finger at him and mumbled in the strange language she had used before. An arch of sparkling green light sped toward him, a jolt hitting him, sending him spinning. His eyes closed and he was falling, falling.

At daybreak, Noah awoke on the deck of the *Mystic Mermaid*. He glanced at the Timex circling his wrist, five-thirty a.m. *What*? He sat up and discovered his missing, waterlogged Nike sat next to him on deck.

"Ahoy, Noah, hit the bottle a little too hard last night?" Oscar chuckled, leaning against a dock piling.

"Hell no, had a little wine at a friend's house. Didn't sleep much either. Sure as hell don't remember lying down on deck to sleep." He rubbed a hand over his face, more than a little puzzled. He recalled grabbing his mackinaw, a cup of coffee, and going on deck. The woman or apparition was on the beach. He followed her, assumed the nymph was Ella and boom; here he was on his boat, with his missing Nike. Was he going crazy? Why couldn't he remember how he got here?

Noah held up his dripping tennis shoe. "You know anything regarding this soaking wet shoe?"

Oscar raised his eyebrows and snorted. "Now what would I know about a sopping wet tennis shoe?"

"Couple of days ago my shoe disappeared." Noah turned the shoe upside down and poured out salt water and a small crab. "Yet here it is back on board." He reached down scooped up the crab and tossed the crustacean overboard.

Oscar narrowed his eyes. "Look here, young fella, I don't mess with what isn't mine. If you're hinting you think I had something to do with your shoe disappearing, you need to think again."

"Nah, Oscar, I'm not accusing you. Did you see anyone hanging around my boat?" Frustrated, Noah flung his shoe against the bait box, where it hit and thumped to the deck. "Someone put my shoe back on the boat."

"Nope. Never saw anyone messing with your boat or your shoe." Oscar said. He looked toward shore a big smile brightened his face. "There's my girl and my pot of chili."

"What girl? What chili?" Noah brushed his windblown hair out of his eyes.

"Ella cooked me dinner," Oscar said. He ran his hand over his grizzled white hair and tucked his shirt into the aged leather belt holding up his denims. "I fixed her truck the other night. She promised me chili and cornbread. The girl is a whiz in the kitchen."

Ella? Noah leaped over the side of the boat and strode up the dock toward Ella, who emerged from her truck with a blue towel wrapped around a big pot. He'd get some answers about the beach, the woods—she'd been there. The nymph was connected to Ella, or she was the nymph, crazy as that seems, he thought.

She closed the door and turned, nearly knocking him down.

He took the towel wrapped pot of chili from her. Breathing in the spicy aroma elicited a rumble from his stomach. "I'll help." Could surprise be making her eyes shine?

"Thanks, I'll grab the cornbread." She hesitated before opening the door back up.

"Ella, last night…" He stared at her baffled look.

Her lips parted in surprise. "It was just a kiss." She spoke softly.

Her emerald green eyes sparkled. She'd pulled her long hair in a ponytail that hung down to her waist and the hairdo only served to emphasize her beautiful eyes and luscious mouth. His fingers ached to release said ponytail and run his fingers through her silken hair.

"A nice kiss," he agreed. How should he broach the subject of the sea nymph without her thinking him completely crazy? Maybe this wasn't the right time. He shifted the pot, the lid let out a small clink.

"Yes, nice." She started down the gravel path toward the dock.

He fell in behind her, watching her long skirt hugging her legs in the light sea breeze. She didn't look like the green enchantress from his dream. Yet something familiar in her shape and the sound of her voice made him swear if the nymph wasn't her, she was a close relative. If there were a sea nymph and not his mind playing tricks on him.

They agreed to meet after work around six in this evening, and all share a meal on Oscar's boat. Noah wasn't sure if he could wait ten hours to see her again.

He cleaned the head, made his bunk and wrote out a shopping list. An ocean breeze had kicked up; he'd need a jacket for town. He opened the wardrobe door. Something wasn't right. His red and black plaid mackinaw was gone, his favorite coat, a present from his Dad. The jacket wasn't on deck or anywhere in the cabin. Had his mackinaw fallen overboard last night like his wayward Nike? Scenes of yesterday played back in his mind. He'd last had his mackinaw in the woods. An icy finger of dread cruised up his spine and lifted the tiny hairs on his neck. What better proof did he need, than finding his mackinaw in the woods?

He grabbed a windbreaker and slammed the door on his way out. He trudged the length of the dock, jogged along the beach around a rock outcropping, took note where he had fallen on the sand, still indented by his knees and hands. He jogged up the slippery dunes, and then across to the forest. In places, the wind had danced around his footprints and hers. There were enough still visible he had a path to track.

Birds chirped overhead. A crow scolded him for intruding into his domain. He slowed to a walk, panting now; a few yards ahead he spotted his jacket neatly folded sitting on a boulder. He simply stared for a moment. Huh? He had flung the jacket, not stopped and folded it.

Snatching up his jacket, he headed towards Shell Cottage.

# # #

Over breakfast, Ella mused, last night she'd almost revealed her Magick to the captain. She was relatively certain the spell she sent hurling toward Noah would leave him with no memory of seeing her in the manifestation of a sea witch.

She answered e-mail from the institute sponsoring her research. Director Hansen wanted to know if her reef project showed signs of growing on the art frame work. She promised pictures and headed outside to take them, first making tea in a heavy mug to stave off the chilly air.

The lab door was a wreck. The hair on her neck prickled with alarm. The lock had been knocked off. Grooves ran six feet high on the door, scratched through the paint down to bare steel. A shiver traced up her spine.

She reached out sending her extra-sensory power into the building; whatever had been in her lab was gone. How had an intruder breached her protection spell? Whoever or whatever had entered must possess a supernatural power strong enough to break her protection spell. She listened for sounds from inside but didn't hear any. Her heart raced as she pushed the door open.

She flipped on the overhead fluorescent lights and took inventory of the damage. Her heart sank. Glass beakers lay shattered on the floor. Microscopes were tipped over.

Repairing those would be expensive if they were damaged, she contemplated, shaking her head. All labeled microarray slides were gone. A week's worth of investigative work had disappeared and she'd have to start over.

For whatever reason, the intruder had not touched any of her reef-building projects. The same couldn't be said for her ocean research endeavor for Poseidon.

The Bunsen burner had landed upright on the floor and the blue flame danced, and thank goodness for that. She stooped and turned the gas jet off. Why would anyone want to demolish her lab? Tongs and crucibles were scattered across the floor.

She dialed the sheriff and explained the situation. Within twenty minutes, the sheriff arrived to take a report while his assistant dusted for fingerprints. They left and she began to clean up. Ella needed to find out who wrecked-havoc in her lab. She swept up broken glass, wondering who had the power to break her spell.

Fingering the key ring in her pocket, she made her decision. After returning the broom to the closet, she unlocked the olive green metal cabinet where she stored Magick dust, potions, and various other Magical items. She picked up the turquoise glass bottle containing Magick dust and set it on the lab table. She swept the floor with her besom, a little broom made from twigs of the sacred hemlock tree, thus sweeping away any negative energy left behind by the intruder. Pushing residual energy from the area, east to west, and south to north she would sweep all destructive energy, shoving unwanted energy out of the space, all the while chanting:

East, south, west, north;
Cleanse this space henceforth,
Protect this circle from the revival,
When pulling the past from the archival
So mote it be.

Holding the uncorked bottle of Magick dust near the floor she walked in a circle eight feet in diameter. She set boundaries using the charmed dust, cleaning and consecrating the area giving her self-protection within the circle. Witch energy she needed to raise in herself and would be contained in the circle until she released it. Grabbing a lab stool, she sat in the middle of the circle. Morning sun peeked in through the windows located along the eaves and coated her in a golden glow. She turned toward the sun closed her eyes, and raised her arms to the Goddess.

Casting out a spell of finding, she murmured in the language of old. Safe in her circle, she opened her eyes and the lab was exactly as she had left it last night.

The door swung open with a bang as it hit the wall. A tall, weasel-looking man, hair stringy and disheveled, entered her workroom. An evil smile adorned his constricted face. He looked familiar, but she couldn't remember where she had seen him.

He methodically went around her lab breaking beakers, throwing tools, and at one point trying to tip over the heavy metal table leaning against the far wall. Bile rose in her throat as he tore her precious lab apart. His destruction was thorough. He grabbed slides off the microscopes, and the cataloged ones in her file box, and put them in his pocket. No, stop, she screamed in her silent bubble of magick. All her work was gone.

He swung an arm out aggressively, knocking over the microscopes. Heat rose up her neck, how dare he, touch her precious microscopes. She'd track him down, find him, and he'd be sorry for ever coming to her lab. Nails from her clenched hands dug into her palms.

As he passed by her circle, he stared right through her. His demonic black eyes seemed to look deep into her soul, even though she was protected and he couldn't see her. Filled with terror, her stomach knotted.

At the door, he turned to survey his handiwork, and in a flash of Magick he was gone. The spell broke, leaving Ella exhausted. Her witch energy burst forth from the circle, swirled around the lab like a sea-green sparkling meteorite with a long tail, it climbed higher and higher slowly vanishing, leaving behind a few sparkles of dust that fell to the floor. She fell from the stool, exhausted from holding on to the Magick for so long. She lay down and stared at the ceiling, trying to get her breath and emotions under control.

Magick in her body tingled and stirred deep inside, a sensation that reminded her of a battery being recharged. One hundred butterflies flitted around in her stomach, as she strived to calm herself.

Someone was out to sabotage her research. The danger to the ocean was imminent and fast approaching the coast. If the burglar was human he would have no way of knowing the consequences to her. Poseidon was specific what would happen if she didn't find the answer for him.

The trespasser wasn't human, he couldn't be. He had power to be able to break her spell.

Finally she sat up, looked around at the mess and decided a little more Magick wouldn't hurt. She raised her hands and began speaking in the old tongue.

"Ella?" Noah said from the doorway, "What are you doing?"

"Yoga?" She dropped her hands to her lap, a nervous laugh escaping.

"What happened in here?" He sounded concerned.

"Someone broke in and destroyed my research. Funny thing though, he took my slides, didn't break them. The ones I showed you. Gone," she said, with a wave of her hand.

He extended a hand to help her up. "Why are you on the floor?" he asked, again. He glanced at the overturned stool. "Did you fall?"

She clasped his hand and stood, her tension eased at the nearness of him. "And you're in my lab why?" Concentrate, Ella, she admonished herself. Magick must be kept in the realm of the Coven, it wouldn't do for the good captain to know, or any uninitiated human, for that matter. There were rules to be followed. Very few humans had knowledge of the Coven.

Evan knew, but he'd been instrumental in saving Hettie from returning to the past when the Warlock Declan tried to take her. Now they were engaged to marry so of course he would know.

No, now was not the time for confessions of being a sea witch.

She slowly withdrew her hand, letting the comforting feeling go. "Well, Captain?" She saw the Mackinaw slung over his shoulder, the one he'd so carelessly thrown off in the woods the previous night. Once she fully morphed, she had retrieved the jacket from the ground, carefully folded it, and set the coat on a boulder.

"I…want to ask you what happened last night," he said.

Her throat constricted. She pretended to mistake his meaning. "The kiss? Again." Shoot! The spell hadn't cleared his memory. She might have expected that; when she tried to work two spells at once, one would sometimes partially cancel the other.

"No, the beach, the woods, and the hemlock tree. You were there, I saw you."

"I have no idea what you mean. Maybe you had a dream?" She moved away, purposely putting space between them.

"Ella, I didn't dream or hallucinate. I chased you." He pointed at her. "Up from the beach and across the dunes, or someone who looked very much like you." He righted her stool. Set his jacket on the seat.

"Maybe you walked in your sleep? And dreamed? For I can assure you I was home in bed." She couldn't bring herself to look him in the eye. She squatted, picked up a heavy stone crucible which had survived the attack, and scooped up other tools lying on the floor, and put them in the bowl. "As you can see, I have quite a mess to take care of, Captain."

He ran his hands through his hair, shaking his head as if trying to get cobwebs out. "Maybe you're right. Maybe I did dream and I did sleepwalk, but it seemed so real."

Her heart ached for him, he sounded so bewildered. "Dreams can trick us. I've had a few dreams I've had a hard time deciphering myself." She placed the crucible on the worktable, sat her microscopes up, and made a mental note to check them over further later. Bit by bit, piece by piece she worked her way around her beloved lab, picking up a tool here, a beaker there and tidying up as she went.

He followed her around, helping put things to right. "Are we still on for tonight, chili, at Oscar's?"

She turned, nearly running into his broad chest. "Of course, I'll be there."

"I'll pick you up."

"Not necessary, Captain." She stuffed her hands into the pockets of her lab coat.

"Oh, but it is, especially since your lab has been broken into."

He wasn't going to settle for *no*; it was written in the set of his face.

"Okay. I'll be ready at six o'clock." Anything to get him out of here and on his way; she had calls to make.

He reached out and unexpectedly squeezed her shoulder. "See you soon." He closed the door on his way out.

Ella stared at the closed door for a few minutes. Tears welled in her eyes that he cared for her safety. His concern touched her heart. The cell vibrated in her pocket. "Hello?"

A man said, "Give up your research on the ocean. The die off of vegetation is going to happen. You can't stop me." Cold as ice, his voice sent chills sliding along her spine.

"Who are you?" Her stomach rolled; witch's intuition told her the caller was the intruder. The same evil energy came through on his voice.

"It doesn't matter. A pity if you lost everything you've worked so hard for. But I can arrange it if you don't back off."

Click and he was gone. What was she going to do? If the caller was the same man from her vision, clearly he could make good on his threats. She was tired of being harassed.

The vision and voice, she tapped a finger against her chin. She'd heard him before, but where?

She dialed Hettie and explained what had happened. "I don't know if he is human or supernatural, but I'm leaning toward supernatural. Hettie, he broke the protection spell! What can we do to stop him from coming back?"

"I'll talk to Darla. Inform her of the intruder," Hettie said. "I want to know what you are going to do about Noah. Casting your spell last night to completely wipe his memory of the episode, didn't work. He told Evan on the phone about last night. Evan told him it was probably a dream since he hadn't been sleeping well lately."

"He's picking me up tonight for dinner at Oscar's. I'll see what I can do to change his recollection of last night. You know what happens when you try to do two spells at once. I sent him back to his boat at the same time I tried to wipe his memory. I'm hopeful he decides he was sleepwalking and dreaming." Fingers crossed and a little spell to ensure the captain wouldn't bring up last night's events at dinnertime.

"Call you later," Hettie said.

"Bye"

Ella changed her cell mode to camera and walked to the back of the building, where miraculously nothing had been destroyed. She took pictures of the art work from different angles. Growing colonies of ocean life were beginning to take form on the art structures. Soon she would be able to test her theory by placing the first works of art on the ocean floor. Her dream would be fulfilled for a living underwater art museum.

Clicking the gallery on her phone, she sent them one by one to her home computer.

After filing paperwork due to the grant foundation, she threw herself into cleaning. Physical work always helped her find her balance, and her stress level was super high today.

By the time she was seated at her desk, late afternoon sun filtered through the lace curtains catching dust fairies in the beams of light. She brought up the screen to examine the pictures. She inserted the first three into the e-mail for the director.

She brought up the fourth photo. Her hands fell to her lap. What she was seeing wasn't possible. The bottom left corner of the photo was hazy but a shiny eye stared out from the shadows under the display table. *What the ...?* Maybe a reflection of Snow's eye; the big cat sometimes followed Ella into the lab. *But one eye?*

She glanced around to see Snow fast asleep on the rocker. She remembered the caterwauling from the other night; had some animal gotten inside her lab?

Not knowing what to expect she picked up her wand and broom, which were equally embedded with Magick from nature. No animal would attack her while she held these.

She flipped on all the lights in the lab. Making her way around the room she followed her instincts, checking under tables, looking for signs an animal was in here, or had been. Finally reaching the display table at the back of the building, and aimed her wand underneath.

Something shiny winked at her from the floor. She bent down and picked up, a knobby button or fastener of some sort, black thread still attached.

"Wherever did this button come from?" She touched the tip of one finger to the worn engraving on the top of the fastener. After scrutinizing the old button, she laid the button on a slide to examine.

She turned on the microscope light. The slide under the scope, she adjusted the magnification until the fine outlines of gold glowed along the grooves of a raised trident design. The elevated trident had long ago lost its luster of gold and now the silver under coat showed through. The motif, though worn, was discernible. She had seen the same button as a decoration on a pea coat jacket, many years ago. But where?

She picked the button up, held it tight and closed her eyes concentrating. The last time she had seen a similar button, was when she attended the air locked underwater academy in Atlantis for one year, during high school.

Kenn, bastard son of Poseidon, had showed her his coat, he was so proud of the fact Poseidon had allowed him into the academy, and given him the jacket. The only recognition Poseidon would ever show toward Kenn.

How did his button end up here in her lab?

Chapter Seven

When Noah arrived that evening the door to Ella's lab was open. He found Ella bent over her microscope. "Still at work?" he asked.

Startled she almost knocked over a beaker which sat near the edge of the work table.

Damn, he had scared her. "Sorry didn't mean to alarm you."

She smiled, tentatively. "I'm fine, a little jumpy after last night's break in." Gesturing toward her microscope, she said, "I'm trying to recreate the same parameters on my tests as before." She removed a slide from the scope and placed it in the file box. "At any rate, I've done all I can for today." She switched off the microscope light and approached him. He held the door open for her following her out and closing the door behind him. He watched as she secured the new lock.

"Time for dinner, Captain. I have to freshen up a bit. I don't have cable, only a DVD player. I never seem to have time to watch T.V., but there are plenty of magazines to entertain you." She led the way across the driveway to a flagstone path leading up to her house.

Man, he hoped she had magazines, anything but scientific ones. Reading over the documents she had given him last night had just almost fried his brain.

"Make yourself at home. I won't be long."

Something was different; she had boxed up all her magazines that had been stacked ten or fifteen deep on the table. Now the ones which had lined the walls were in magazine boxes too, clearly labeled by type and year. Boxes lined the wall but in a much more orderly fashion than the chaotic stacks from last time he had visited.

The focal point of her small living room was a stone faced fireplace. He studied the stone and ran his hand over rough gray rock, stopping to examine sea shells stuck into mortar here and there filling the space between the stones. There were northern moon shells, their butterscotch wavy lines danced in the lamplight. Amethyst Gem Clam, the white coloring suffused in purple, and limpets, their simple broad conical shell, and many more. The hearth was a fitting tribute to Shell Cottage and the coastal town of Waxing.

Noah pulled out a wooden chair and sat at the round oak table. Shell Cottage was a comfortable cottage, he decided. He spotted her radio and CD player and got up to take a closer look.

"Do you mind if I turn the CD player on?" he asked.

"Music would be lovely," she said, from the bedroom. "I put a couple of CDs on earlier today. You only have to turn it on."

The strains of an Irish ballad filled the room, harmonious string sounds of harps and guitars, music that made him smile, light and airy, a happy tune.

The room suited Ella. He wandered into the little kitchen where a stack of dirty dishes sat on the counter.

"Ah, well," he said, as he set the dishes in the sink and turned on the tap water. He squeezed dish soap into the hot water that filled the sink.

That's how she found him, up to his elbows in soapy water. Exasperation colored her tone. "Do you always wash other people's dishes?"

"Pet peeve of mine, I can't pass up dirty dishes." He opened the drain and wrung out the wet dishcloth. When he turned, Ella stood before him leaving him speechless. Her green flowered ankle length dress was beautiful, but the off shoulder sleeves, exposed her beautifully toned smooth shoulders, very kissable shoulders, that is what did him in. He was an idiot. He couldn't take his eyes off her.

Amusement flickered in her eyes. "Thank you for doing my dishes."

At last he found he could speak. "You look nice." His mouth was dry as cotton. Nice? Hell, she was beautiful. "Shall we go?"

#

Dinner was quick and easy. Oscar insisted on doing the dishes and said an early goodnight to Ella and Noah, shooing them off the *Red Moon*. Oscar wanted to be at the Northern fishing grounds before sunrise tomorrow.

"Would you like a cup of coffee before I take you home?" This was probably a crazy thing to do, but he had been thinking of last night's kiss all evening. He wanted to get to know Ella better, maybe even steal another kiss.

"Sure." A sea breeze had kicked up and was on the blustery side, now pushing a fog bank closer. She pulled her woven green shawl closer. He extended his hand and helped her onto his boat.

"Do you want a jacket?" Noah offered.

"I'm okay for now."

He went below to brew coffee. The tide had turned and was coming in. Small waves lapped against the boat, definitely the most soothing sound he could imagine.

By the time they had settled down in deck chairs, and with mugs of coffee to warm their hands, the wind had relaxed to a light breeze.

"I'd like to take you out on my boat sometime." He'd like to tomorrow. "I'll be fishing once I get my new permit. I expected it to arrive yesterday, but no such luck."

"Yes, I'd like to go," she said eagerly. "In fact, I have a proposition for you."

"Proposition?" he chuckled. "I'd like to hear it." Her cheeks bloomed a shade of pink same as the 'Angel Face' roses growing in her garden.

Laughter reached her eyes. "Oh, not that kind! I need to collect samples for my research. Is the continental rise far from here? I want to hire you to take me there. What do you think, Captain?"

"Sure I'll take you, but you're not paying me. Consider this trip a favor. I might need one someday. Should take three hours out and three back." He rubbed the back of his neck. Ella on his boat for more than six hours could be good or bad. One thing for sure, he'd get to know her better. "We could head out at eight o'clock, be back around three. Would that time framework for you?"

"Yes. How exciting. I've never been out on a boat." She clapped her hands, a look of pure joy spreading across her face. She looked at him as if she were seeing him for the first time. "I like you, Captain."

Noah didn't get his kiss, he got something better—a date, sort of, with Ella. He walked her home and whistled on his way back to the *Mystic Mermaid*.

# # #

Oscar's slip was empty when Noah woke up the next morning. He tidied up the galley, stateroom, and checked the head for toilet paper. Flipping switches on, he did his usual pre-voyage check. He put the engine in idle and let it warm up. Fuel was good, he had filled up yesterday, and oil pressure was fine, bilge pump was discharging.

All gear was stored so there was plenty of room on deck for their excursion.

The miasma swirled around the bay, giving an otherworldly feel to the morning. Her footsteps reached his ears before she materialized out of thick fog. He reached up and took a blue leather barrel satchel from her, and almost dropped it. "Whoa, I didn't expect this bag to be so heavy. What do you have in here, all your shoes?"

Ella laughed with such great musicality. "These are tools of my trade and a few research books."

She took his offered hand and stepped lightly onto the deck. "Quite a chill in the air this morning, I wasn't expecting it." She shifted the matching blue backpack resting on her shoulder and smiled, sending his pulse racing.

"Go down below." He pointed toward the gangway steps. "The heater is on. Coffee is made; help yourself."

He undid the bowline and prepared to cast off. Once they were underway, she brought him a cup of coffee. "So first time on the ocean—did you take Dramamine?"

He blasted his horn one long blast and two short, repeating every two minutes until the boat emerged from the shore-hugging fog.

The distant coastline was hidden away by clinging miasma; a steel blue ocean, on the other hand, went on and on till sea melded into a dove gray sky.

They rode in silence, with only the slap of waves hitting against the boat and the motor surging them ahead through frothy whitecaps.

"I had no idea being on the surface of the ocean could be so calming." Ella closed her eyes and breathed deeply. She looked like a ship's figurehead leaning against the rail. Her head was thrown back and her dress molded to her slender figure by the breeze.

"On the surface?" He wrinkled his brow; she had a funny way of articulating things sometimes.

"Oh, you know," she waved her hand, "on a boat, on the ocean."

How could she not have been on a boat? Wasn't she an oceanographer or something?

Thick, gray-black clouds gathered on the horizon to the northeast derailed that line of thought. Noah cursed their bad luck. "We'll go inside in a few minutes. Looks like we're headed for a squall." Steel skies turned the water a dark angry gray.

Ten minutes later and the squall battered them. The boat lumbered against wind and wave. "This storm is moving fast," Noah said, checking his instruments.

"What can I do?" Ella grasped hold of the back of his captain's chair inside the cabin.

"Hang on tight; we'll have to ride this storm out." His grip tightened on the wheel. He headed his boat into the next wave. The wave curled and broke over the bow. For a few seconds, their view was obstructed by foamy water. So far the swells were of a manageable size. But fear bit at the back of his neck.

Ella shrieked. Noah's forearms bulged under the strain of keeping his boat on course. Sweat ran down his back. Maybe he shouldn't have brought Ella out. If anything happened to her—well, he didn't even want to think about that possibility.

Several more troughs and waves passed before the boat broke free of the storm.

He couldn't believe how short lived the squall was. He thought about the day Bruce died and Noah's first vessel *Lure of the C* sank. That squall had come on fast and left just as fast, an extra-large rogue wave claiming his boat and Bruce, pulling his friend down to the icy depths of the Atlantic.

She laid her hand on his arm. "It's over. What is troubling you?"

He shrugged. "Lost *Lure of the C,* my boat, and Bruce in exactly a storm like we passed through a few minutes ago," he said the weight of a steel anchor in his chest. He glanced at her; she was so composed. "Are you still glad you came?"

"Oh, yes. Being in the storm was exhilarating. Except that first wave over the bow; I wasn't expecting it." She shuddered. "Tell me about the storm, when *Lure of the C* sank." She sat down in the mate's chair. "How did you survive?"

"By chance and a mermaid." He watched her, expecting laughter.

Ella didn't even blink. "I want the whole story, Captain, because if you hadn't survived you and I wouldn't be sitting here. It must have been a miracle." She angled her head to the side an encouraging smile touched her lips.

"The rogue wave broke over the bow, hard and fast like the ones we experienced a while ago, except ten times more powerful. This wave was twenty feet higher and came at an angle to all the others, skewering my boat on its side." Sweat was gathering on his brow; he wiped at it with his shirtsleeve. "The wave killed the engines and we were left to be tossed and turned." He took a deep breath and exhaled. "I radioed 'Mayday' and our position. My boat was sinking fast. The holding tank doors popped open. In a matter of minutes our empty tank filled with water and *Lure of the C* listed on her side." He glanced at Ella, her eyes glistened with tears. "We threw our life raft in the water and...jumped."

"And Bruce?"

"His foot tangled in some line." He rubbed the back of his neck. "Bruce went down with the boat. I searched, dove deep looking for him. The boat had disappeared in the dark depths of the sea, taking Bruce to his death."

"Were you able to get to the lifeboat?" Ella moved closer to him.

"The lifeboat...had disappeared in the high swells, never saw it again."

Noah rubbed his jaw. "Here is where my story gets crazy. The gale was short lived, and I floated on my back after I became too exhausted to swim. I felt a nudge on my shoulder, turned out to be a large wooden pallet. I was too weak to climb up and the pallet kept floating away from me. By then I was too exhausted to care, I was giving in to the cold."

He turned to gaze into Ella's eyes. He wanted to gauge her reaction. "I'll swear on a stack of Bibles when I looked toward the pallet, a pink haired mermaid was pushing that pallet back toward me. She helped me get up on it." He fiddled with the Saint Christopher medal hanging around his neck. "She never said a word, helped me though, a bemused smile on her lips. As she dove underwater, her iridescent tail slapped like a whale's. And she was gone."

Instead of laughing at him, Ella looked both puzzled and amazed.

"You're not laughing." Did she actually believe him?

"No, I'm not." She smiled. "There are things in our universe not easily explained. I think the mermaid who rescued you is one of those incidences. Were you far from here when the storm struck?"

How could she be so matter of fact concerning his mermaid story?

The radio crackled before he could form a response. "Mayday! Mayday! This is the *Red Moon,* Oscar Aldrich…taking on water…" The radio continued to crackle.

Noah grabbed the microphone from his Marine Radio. "Oscar! Noah Drago here, what's your position, over?"

Noah wrote down Oscar's coordinates. "He must have run into the squall we came through. I'm heading back—I won't let this sea claim another friend." He steered his boat back the way they had come, chasing after the storm.

Gray clouds were leaden, almost black, and towered above the horizon. The hull slapped against waves, the sea churned beneath them.

Soon a blinding fog swirled around the boat, making it impossible to see, let alone find Oscar's boat. Noah eased up on the throttle when they approached the coordinates Oscar had given. Ella went out on deck. The boat rocked up and down on angry waves.

He glanced over his shoulder. She stood on the aft deck. "Ella, come back inside!" The sea tried to wrench the wheel from his hands. He struggled to control the helm.

He looked again and she had raised her hands toward the sky. Clouds parted, the sun broke through encircling the boat. The seas calmed, flattened, identical to a lake on a summer day. He couldn't believe what he was seeing. The squall continued to rage around their circle of calm.

"Oscar!" Ella cried, pointing to starboard.

She dove into the water. Noah cut the engines and ran to look over the side, nothing. His hands were clammy, no, no, not another loss. He searched the waters for any sign of Ella or Oscar.

Finally, he saw them, one hundred yards behind and to the starboard. Ella tried to help Oscar onto a floating ice chest. She swam and pushed him toward Noah.

When they were close enough, Noah threw out two life preservers. Oscar slipped off the ice chest and grabbed a life preserver. Ella swam toward the other one. Noah pulled Oscar over to the side of the boat. He helped Oscar aboard. Grabbing a coverlet, and wrapping the soft blanket over the crusty sailor's shoulders.

"I lost the *Red Moon*. She's gone!" Oscar sobbed, his shoulders shaking.

Noah looked over the side of the boat; he couldn't see Ella anywhere. The second life preserver floated empty. "Ella, Ella!"

He kicked off his shoes and jumped overboard. Deeper and deeper he swam until he thought his lungs would rupture. At last she swam toward him out of the deep dark blue of the ocean. She smiled, took his hand, and a burning sensation shot through his hand and up his arm. *What was that?* They rose toward the surface together.

Only they weren't together. She had let go. His hand was numb from the cold water and he hadn't felt her slip away.

He broke through the surface of the sea gasping for breath like a fish out of water. Treading water, he looked for her. "Ella! Ella!" Frantic, when she didn't respond. He dove below again, searching.

She was sinking back toward the bottom. He swam the ten yards that separated them and grabbed her to him, holding her limp form close. He kicked toward the surface.

Oscar helped them aboard. Noah laid Ella on the deck. When he brushed her hair back off her face, he saw a dusting of green scales.

"My eyes are old but I'm not color blind. What's wrong with our girl? She's barely breathing, and her color should be blue, not green from lack of oxygen," Oscar said, his face a mask of bewilderment.

Noah brought a blanket off his bunk and gently draped it over her still form.

"I'm not sure," Noah said, but he would find out. She *was* his mystery beach nymph, now he was convinced. She wasn't the pink haired mermaid who saved his life though. How many unknown creatures lived in the ocean and on land, for that matter?

Her eyes were closed, her breathing shallow. He tucked the blanket around her and carried her to his bunk.

Oscar came inside, throwing an arm around Noah's shoulder. "Thanks for coming after me." He gave Noah a squeeze. "Now let's see about getting through this storm and to home port safely."

"I checked NOAA before we left. All that was predicted was possible light rain." Noah glanced at Oscar.

"Same here."

They both stared out the cockpit window in awe. The mother of all storms was headed their way. Noah started the engine as a frenzied wind kicked up the waves and roiling clouds of steel raced to meet them.

Chapter Eight

Ella was jarred awake by the bow slamming down on the onslaught of waves. Thunder booming overhead was so loud she couldn't hear what Oscar and Noah were talking about. Lightning flashed and a crash of thunder peeled on its heels directly overhead. The sky was so dark it looked like late evening, but a clock on the wall showed one o'clock in the afternoon.

She sat up on the edge of the bunk. A little dizzy, she felt for her gills and found they had disappeared. Iridescent green scales still dusted her arms. She raked her hand through her tangled mess of hair. No longer blonde her waist long lengths lay across her hand still tinted green. *Oh, dear. How will I explain my hair?*

"Feeling better?" Noah stood in the doorway.

"Yes, much," she said, forcing a smile she really didn't feel. "Thanks for coming back for me."

He kneeled in front of her, eyebrows furrowing. "Ella, I need an explanation."

"Not now." She looked away and gulped forcing down the queasiness in her stomach, not wanting to meet his intense gaze.

"Soon?"

"Soon, I promise."

She raised her hand to cup his cheek, but he grabbed her hand instead. "No more tricks. I'm not sure how you did it, but you pointed your finger at me in the woods, I ended up back on my boat, and I thought the whole episode was a dream." He fingered her hair. "I don't understand what is going on. Still, your hair is a lovely shade of green," he said, a tentative smile gracing his face. He laid her hand on top of the blanket. "Rest Ella, I'm needed in the wheel house."

Ella watched him leave and reclined back on the bunk. She wished the spinning in her head would stop. Drifting in and out of sleep, she relived her and Oscar's rescue.

# # #

When Oscar's Mayday call had come in, Ella's pulse had raced. She had to do something. Noah wouldn't reach Oscar in time to save him. She went out on deck and raised her arms in supplication to the goddess who in turn fought on their behalf for calm seas. What she got was a small area of tranquil water, windless and flat, while the squall continued to rage around the vessel.

She spotted Oscar hanging onto an ice chest. He slipped off and managed to hang on to the handles, but he was getting weaker by the moment. Frigid waters in the north Atlantic would drive him to hypothermia in only a few more minutes.

She dove in, only afterward thinking of the consequences of beginning her metamorphosis *after* going in the ocean. She managed to swallow a bucket of seawater before her gills started working.

James! I need your help. She could only hope he was close enough to get her message. He would have sped her along. Swimming on her own, she wasn't nearly as fast. She pushed Oscar from underwater toward the boat. Her gills were working, but not efficiently. She was weak. Her scales, a sure sign she had changed, had not materialized on her arms. One final push toward the safety of the boat and Oscar was within reach of one of two life preservers floating on the surface. Oscar grabbed one close to him.

She was rapidly sinking into the depths again. It felt like she was being sucked under, completely out of control. She tried to swim but something was amiss—her physical change was not complete and left her with little power in the ocean. A splash and Noah was swimming down for her. His brow wrinkled, as his powerful arms drove him closer. *Noah is coming for me.* She smiled, finding amusement in a human trying to save a witch.

What are you doing so far from shore unaided? James' voice boomed in her head.

I was on Noah's boat. Oscar fell in and I had no choice but to save him.

The octopus wrapped a tentacle around her and pushed her toward Noah. *Swim, darling, don't make me expose myself to the human.*

Thanks, James.

She swam upward, till her hand grasped Noah's. As they touched a jolt of power between them shocked her. She gasped. He pulled her upwards toward the surface. Her fingers slipped out of his and she sunk again. The last thing she remembered was Noah swimming down toward her.

#

Hours later they arrived back dockside; Noah had radioed ahead was thankful to see Hettie and Evan waited for them.

Ella had not completely changed back, and the queasy roll of her stomach was not a good sign.

Hettie ran to her. "Oh, you look awful." She threw her arms around Ella. "Your hair is still green," she whispered.

"I know. Something went dreadfully wrong when I jumped in to save Oscar. We need to talk. I feel…" Her knees gave out and she slumped against Hettie.

"Noah!" Hettie yelled, somehow supporting her weight.

Noah jumped up onto the dock and scooped Ella up. "Where to, Hettie?"

"Take her to my place, the Crystal Witch, upstairs."

"Oscar? Are you okay?" Noah said, before leaving.

"Go on, I'll batten down the hatches and take care of your boat." Oscar waved them off.

"Make yourself at home," Noah offered. "There's plenty of food in the fridge and dry bedding in the hatch above the bunk. Sleep here tonight."

"Don't worry, mate, I'll make myself at home. Right after I call my insurance company." He took his stub of a cigar out of his pocket. "I'm gonna miss old *RedMoon*. She's been my lady for more years than I care to count." He sniffled and wiped his face on his coat sleeve.

"Is Ella gonna be all right?" Oscar choked out.

Was she? Ella wondered.

She'd never gone into the water before her metamorphous was complete.

Hettie turned to her and murmured an incantation. "She'll be fine, Oscar. She's a little waterlogged is all."

Evan clapped Noah on the back. "Glad everyone's okay. I'll stay and help Oscar. Go take care of your lady."

"Thanks."

His lady, Evan had called her; she could get used to being Noah's lady. Ella pressed her ear to his chest. He cared for her. She could tell by the rhythmic drumming of his heart. She didn't mind being taken care of, she was exhausted. Her eyes drifted shut.

Later that evening she woke to a delicious aroma of Bergamot filling the air, of course, Earl Grey tea. Always a good eye opener, she sat up to find herself in bed. Ella took the cup of tea from Hettie.

"You've got an anxious fella waiting downstairs to see you." Hettie smiled.

"Hettie, he saw me during my change. Oscar did too."

"I've taken care of Oscar. He doesn't remember your scales or green hair." Hettie took a handful of hair and gave a playful tug. "Blonde again, and you know what? You're gorgeous with green or blonde hair."

"The captain, Noah? Does he remember?"

"Oh, yeah, you've somehow forged a connection with him. Meaning we can no longer wipe his mind clean—none of us in the coven can." Hettie took Ella's hand in hers. "I think the time is here for you to tell Noah what your powers are. Somehow he factors into everything, the research, and the solution. You need to trust him."

Trust a human with her secret? He must find her bizarre, her green scales and hair. Pain shot through her. She arched her back against incredible pain. Her metamorphosis was taking longer than usual. Probably, because she hadn't waited till she'd changed before diving into the sea.

After Hettie left, Ella leaned her head back against a soft cushioned headboard, closed her eyes and focused on breathing in sweet aroma from the tea. She sensed his presence even before he spoke. They had a bond now; the same one Hettie had spoken of. She knew the exact moment their bond was formed. When Noah reached out for her in the ocean, and pulled her back from the depths. When their hands touched she'd felt a jolt pass between them. Hand to hand, heart to heart. They were bonded, truly. She'd make him understand he was now a part of her world. She had no choice, really. If he decided not to be part of her world, hers would be a life without love.

With her eyes still shut, she said, "I guess you want some things clarified?"

"Clarified? Explained? Answers, I want answers, Ella. What the hell is going on?" His tone held a rasp of anger.

She opened one eye and looked at him. "I suppose I owe you that answer now."

"Let's start with your scales and green hair." He sounded frustrated. "Yes, let's start there."

"Do you remember, Captain, when I said there are things in our universe not easily explained?" She set her porcelain cup in the saucer on the nightstand.

"Yes." He came nearer and pulled a wooden chair over to sit on.

"I'm one of those things. I'm a sea witch, which means I survive on land and in the ocean." She might as well get it all out at once. "I answer to Darla, who is the Coastal Coven high witch here in Waxing, but I also answer to Poseidon."

She eased her right leg out from under the feather comforter; gathered up the nightgown Hettie had put on her revealing the trident tattoo on her calf. "When Poseidon requests my presence, my tattoo changes color and throbs."

"What...you're telling me is Poseidon is not a myth, but really exists? You and Darla are witches?" He put his head in his hands, shaking it back and forth. "This is crazy, how can you expect me to believe what you're telling me?"

"Hettie too, she's a witch. Evan knows; he helped save Hettie last year when a Sorcerer, Declan, time traveled to present day Waxing to take her back to the sixteen hundreds."

"Time traveled?" He stood up pacing to the door and back. "This is a lot to take in." He hooked his fingers in his pockets.

"I know. I'm sorry," she said and found she meant it.

"So you can do Magick?"

She raised her hand, summoning her power; all the candles in the room burst into flames.

"Damn! How'd you light those candles?" He walked over to the dresser and held his hand over one. "Ouch!" He jerked his hand away and massaged his palm. "The flames are real?"

"Yes, they are hot too. No black Magick. We don't practice the dark arts." She swung her legs over the side and stood. "We are gray witches. I must beseech you to keep any knowledge of the Costal Coven to yourself. Of course, any questions you have you can ask me, Hettie or Evan."

He took a step backward. "What's a gray witch?"

"We work in conjunction with nature to heal and protect. I work for Poseidon. I'm a guardian of the ocean. One of many guardians." They stood staring at each other in the quiet bedroom. Myths and Magick, witches and sea nymphs, definitely a lot for Noah to take in; the strength of the bond forged between them, pulled her. The wall she had built around her heart had cracked, and crumbled. He didn't know yet, but she was his. She wanted to help him, but how?

She stepped closer till they stood toe to toe. "Let me show you my worlds, both mythical and scientific, please."

"Not right now. I have to…" He gestured toward the door. "There's something I have to do." He backed away, never taking his eyes off her, looking at her as if she were a sea cucumber.

What did he think she would do, jump his bones, or turn him into a frog? This was not going well. "Noah, you saw me the other night in my sea witch form. When I morph I have gills, iridescent green scales on my body, I can endure long periods of time underwater, and my hair is light green."

His hand was on the doorknob. "Do you fly through the air on a broom, or change into a mermaid?"

"No, please, Noah, let me explain." She crossed to him, and with each step her heart shattered further. The sensation of water inside her, normally a balm turned to ice when she saw his rigid posture and the stony look on his face.

"Stop," he held up his hand, palm outward. "Give me time to digest what you've told me." The door shut behind him and he was gone. Sagging against the door she slid down to the floor. She pressed her hands to her temples. She'd scared him away, too much information, or not enough. Tears came like rivers from her eyes and she sobbed so hard she hiccupped.

After a while she got up and looked out the bedroom window. The sky was magnificent; streaks of pink and shades of purple, these last remnants of the storm filled the sky. The beautiful evening sky did nothing for Ella's mood. Today had been long and trying.

Hettie peeked around the door. "I dried your clothes. I thought you might be ready to get dressed."

Ella smiled. "Thanks for taking care of me. Sorry I'm such a burden."

"No burden at all. How did your talk go?"

Ella sighed. "Not good, I'm afraid. He has a lot to think about." She slipped her undergarments on and pulled her long dress over her head. "You are right. We do have a bond. It happened in the ocean, Noah grabbed my hand to pull me to the surface and a surge of power went between us. I didn't realize at the time we had bonded."

"When you placed your trust in Noah to pull you to safety, the connection was initiated. You understand what this signifies?"

"He's my mate, a human. Now all I have to do is convince him we're meant to be together." Ella sat down on the stool in front of the mirrored dresser.

Hettie picked up a brush and groomed Ella's hair in long easy strokes. "You know, sometimes humans need a little time to adjust to the reality of Magick."

"He's not going to like my appearance when I turn. He's seen me, but not in full sea witch mode, at least not up close."

"What's not to like? You are beautiful when you change into a sea witch." Hettie plaited Ella's hair and tied a green grosgrain ribbon on the end of the braid. "You need to embrace that part of yourself. Your skin and hair are stunning. I'm sure Noah merely needs time to mull over all this information, come to terms with the whole idea. Now, gather your things. I'll drive you home."

# # #

Ella stood in her small kitchen and stirred honey into her calming tea. She had never connected fully with any man. She had enjoyed their company, but never sensed a spark, a connection. Now she understood; she had been waiting for Noah. And she may have lost him before they had a chance. She was definitely connected to him, but she understood Noah, being human, had free choice

There are many reasons their relationship couldn't, wouldn't work.

The May sun broke free of the clouds and slid behind the pines trees in the forest. Night brought thoughts of the intruder. She shuddered, knowing someone had violated her lab, her space. "Well, Snow, you want to come? I'm going to check my lab, make sure it's secure for the night."

The cat jumped down from the rocker, stretched and followed Ella to the door. The darkness of the night was on them now and a light breeze kicked up small bits of sand. Wisps of hair had escaped her braid and tickled her cheek.

The outside motion lights came on, and flooded the yard in light. A loud howl quite close sent her hurrying toward safety; she wasted no time opening the lab door. Once she and Snow were safely within, she locked the door and set a protection spell.

The view through her microscope showed the experiments were back on track. She checked her reef growth projects and was pleased to see invertebrates were attaching nicely to the artwork. Soon she'd place the first art piece on the bottom of the Atlantic, off Turtle Point.

The metal building creaked and groaned as heat from the day left the structure. Chills ran up her arms. She walked to the back of the building and shined her flashlight into corners, under the tables. Everything appeared to be in order. No strange varmints lurking inside. She cast a spell, protecting the building from intruders.

"Come on, kitty, let's go."

Back inside the cottage she had a strong sensation someone watched her. Darkness from outside pressed in upon her through the windows. She walked around with clammy hands and closed all curtains and drapes. Terrible to be frightened in my own home, she thought, and she double-checked all locks on the doors, making sure there was no counter spell.

Music would be nice. Grabbing her remote for the CD player, she turned on the music. Music Noah had played burst forth in a merry tune. She smiled in spite of herself. The captain had never listened to Irish music, and yet he had enjoyed doing so the other night.

She sat at her desk and powered up her computer. For the next hour she answered e-mails from the grant foundation. Part of her job was to answer questions from the public about her project. The more people knew, the more likely they would be inclined to donate to the foundation. She didn't mind really, and rather enjoyed the interaction with interested folks.

Ding.

Incoming mail; she would look at one more before bed she decided.

Doctor Stone,

Forget looking for the cause of the flora and fauna die off. If you continue in pursuit, there will be severe consequences.

Count this as your last warning. I know you started your experiment up again. Destroy it. If you care what happens to your friends and your reef research project, you will stop now.

I'm watching.

Chapter Nine

Noah left the Crystal Witch shop and drove up the coast. He had a lump in his throat the size of an orange. He didn't know what to believe. Ella a witch, and not only a witch but an amphibian witch who swims in the sea and turns green? And Hettie a time-traveling witch? How many more witches were there? He shook his head in disbelief. Evan knew everything in regard to this Magick business and had never said a word to him.

He drove till sunset before turning around. He headed back toward Waxing. At Turtle Point he turned off the highway, and killed the engine. He leaned his forehead against the steering wheel. Fatigue hit him like a fast-moving storm. What a day.

He needed answers. The responses he got from Ella only raised more questions. He stared out at the ocean and endless blackness. Lowering the window, Noah sat listening to the sound of waves colliding against rocks at the bottom of the cliff. A light breeze carried the smell of brine in the air. Breathing deep and moisture soothed his raw throat.

Far out to sea, lightning flashed across the blackened sky, a reminder of the horrid squall that came damn near to taking the lives of Ella and Oscar today. Something had happened in the depths of the ocean between Ella and him. When he dove into the sea to pull Ella to the surface, he'd experienced a jolt similar to electricity. How was that possible? Electricity in the water?

He started the car, put the transmission in gear and drove to Evan's house. He sat in his car trying to decide if he should bother Evan or not.

A knock on his car window sent his heart reeling.

"Are you going to sit out here all night?" Evan grinned.

"Didn't know if I should bother you or not." Noah said.

Noah opened the door and they walked together in the direction of the house.

"Lucky you caught me at home. I came by to pick up a few things." He stuck his key in the lock. "I'm staying at Hettie's now, for the most part." His tone was apologetic.

"Hettie tell you about Ella?" He sounded shaky.

Evan looked at him compassion filled his eyes. "Yeah, I know everything. Starting with the coven and ending with Ella's special powers." He clapped a hand on Noah's shoulder. "Hey, buddy, I know your witch coming out of the closet is a shock. I was shocked too, learning Hettie is a witch and belongs to a coven. Come on in. We'll pop a couple beers and talk."

"Best offer I've had all day."

# # #

The next morning, Ella had a few items to pick up in the village. She made a note to stop and see Darla, catch her up on all the latest developments. Anxiety pushed at her heart. Noah, did he come to terms with the whole witch thing? He hadn't called and she wasn't going to call him. This decision was his to make. Would he come to her, be with her? With each hour that passed her hope grew dimmer.

She opened the door to her truck to find a teenage girl, short shocking-pink hair sticking out every which way, sleeping on the seat. Ella shook the girl till she rolled over. Mischell, youngest of four mermaids roaming the waters off the shoreline lay on the front seat, sound asleep. Her hair would turn lime-green when she reached adulthood.

"Mischell, wake up." She shook her harder.

"Hey, watch the shoulder. Aren't you pleased to see me?" Mischell pushed herself up to sitting, stifling a yawn. Her crown of short pink hair stuck out every which way. In human form, she preferred steampunk clothes. Today she sported a black leather bustier decorated with chains, gears and a zipper, black tights and a short black skirt.

"Nice clothes," Ella said, holding in a giggle. Mischell was a typical teenager even if she was a mermaid; she dressed to please herself and no one else.

"Do you like my shoes? James found them for me." Mischell pointed her foot in front of her. Bright sunshine gleamed on silver ballet flats.

"Oh, my, they…are lovely." Her shoes didn't really match her outfit, but Mischell seemed pleased with them. "Why are you here? Your training isn't over for two more years."

"I've evolved enough I can come on land for longer periods of time. James helped me get here." She slid out of the truck. "I'm here to give you a message. James was called away by his lordship, and I'm to check clothing bins at the thrift shop, clothes for me and shoes for James. He is extremely specific on what colors he wants." She counted them off on her fingers. "First he wants purple shoes, preferably sequin, second, black riding boots, third, brown work boots, and yellow shoes, if I can find any. Oh, and only matching pairs." She rolled her eyes.

The odd odor of too many people mixed together reached Ella's nose. "Did you get your clothes from the thrift shop donation bin?"

"No one wanted them, so I took them."

"Mischell, you need to go back in the ocean. You're not through growing. When you stay out of the water there's always a chance you'll change back and die on land."

Silver bracelets jangled against a steampunk gear bracelet as Mischell crossed her arms. "It's not fair. You can come and go whenever you please."

"I'm not a mermaid like you, I'm a sea witch. Do you understand?" Ella squeezed Mischell's shoulder. She'd always had a special spot in her heart for the young mermaid.

Mischell had been banished from Atlantis because she had a desire for shiny pretty things. Unfortunately, some of those things belonged to others. So she was sent here to learn some manners and rules of the ocean. Her training was put in the hands of three other mermaids, who were not thrilled being held responsible for the child. Ella could still remember cries of protest from Mischell when she was taken from the only home she'd ever known, and at such a young age. "How long can you stay?"

"I've only been here a short time, so maybe five hours?" She clasped her hands under her chin, her face glowing with expectation. "Can I stay today, please, please? I won't be any trouble, I promise."

"Okay, for a couple of hours. Now, what message do you have for me from James?"

"He investigated Razor Trench, You know the one you saw the light in. Someone or thing has made a home down there. He couldn't get inside because the trench's sides are unstable. James thinks there is a way in through an underwater cave." Mischell followed Ella inside the cottage. "Do you have any Tootsie Roll Pops?"

"No, I don't but we'll get some." Ella grabbed her purse off the table. "Come on, we'll go to the store. I'm going to stop and see Darla on the way. You remember Darla?"

"She's scary. Do I have to go? Darla's like the super high boss witch, isn't she?"

"Well, I could drop you off at the thrift shop and pick you up after I see Darla." Ella fished a twenty out of her wallet. "Here, I want you to go into the store and shop. No bin diving. If you don't have enough money, we'll discuss it when I get back. Wait for me there, don't go anywhere else, understood?"

"I promise on my collection of rings, bells and cockle shells I won't leave." She tucked the money into her bustier, and with enthusiasm of youth, clapped her hands. "Let's go."

# # #

Ella pulled her old truck into Darla's driveway, turned off the ignition, and looked up to see Darla in the open doorway. Ella had told Noah, a human, Magick existed right here in Waxing, and there was a coven. She ran a hand down her throat, trying to ease her nerves.

She got out and walked toward Darla.

Darla crossed her arms. "I've been waiting for you. Where's your little friend?"

"Mischell?"

"Who else?" Darla opened the door further and stepped back.

"Shopping."

Darla was a witch medium, and her spirit guides kept her up to date on local goings on; not everything, but quite a bit. "The little fishtail is still afraid of me?" Darla asked, her black eyes flashed controlled merriment.

"Yep. You scared her pretty good last time she came ashore."

"For her own good, she has no business being on land. Come on in. We'll have tea and talk."

"I know, but she brought me a message from James. Someone is living in Razor Trench. I spotted a light down in the trench when I visited Poseidon on Monday." Ella swallowed; best to tell Darla her purpose for being here. "I've bonded to Noah."

"And is he happy, glad, indifferent or plain scared out of his wits?" Darla filled the teapot with water, set it on the burner and turned the stove on.

"I don't know. He was shaken up when he left Hettie's last night." She sensed a pull to him even now. Like she should go to him, find him before it was too late. "He hasn't called or stopped by today, I'm afraid he's appalled at the way I look when I change and of course, the fact I'm a witch."

"So he knows you have Magick and the coven exists?" Darla turned a stern face toward her. "Can you wipe his mind?"

"Hettie tried last night, but our bond is too powerful."

"My suggestion to you is to find him. Convince him to keep our secret. We can't let a human wander around Waxing telling others. We would all be in potential danger. We'd have to leave here and start anew somewhere else." Darla poured tea in mugs and set them on the red and white checked tablecloth.

"Understood." Ella sat. "Could you ask Kiki to find Noah?" Kiki was Darla's spirit guide.

"No, you must find him, no one else, convince him. You made this mess by jumping in the water to save Oscar. Your intentions were good, but the results were you exposed your sea witch self to both Noah and Oscar. I have a feeling our good captain will come around."

"I'll find him, talk to him." She wasn't sure how, but she'd convince him they belonged together, for her sake and the sake of the Coastal Coven.

# # #

Back at Shell Cottage, Ella took three Tootsie Roll Pops out of her shopping bag for Mischell.

"Only three?" Mischell pouted, her lower lip sticking out.

"Three is enough. You don't need a sugar high when you have to go back in the ocean."

"Fine, can I at least watch a show till time to go?" Mischell pulled a fake turquoise necklace out of her shopping bag and slipped the string of beads over her head. Next she pulled out four bangle bracelets and slipped them on.

"Sure. Look here, would you like to watch *The Little Mermaid.* I have the DVD?"

Mischell clapped and screamed with delight. "It's my favorite movie! I've only seen it twice. Incredibly adorable!" She dumped her second shopping bag out on the floor to reveal purple shoes and black boots she'd purchase for James. "You think he'll like them?"

"He'll love them. I'll drive you down to Turtle Point in one hour. If you need anything I'll be outside in my lab, okay?"

Her "little mermaid" was completely content, camped on the floor in front of the tube.

She left the lab door open in case Mischell needed her. She slipped into her lab coat, put on her goggles and snapped on latex gloves.

The petri dish samples had doubled in size. The pathogen was getting stronger. She harvested a thin sample for her slide and viewed RTB-1 through her microscope.

"Oh, my." She needed to find a way to stop any more growth. If she couldn't find its source, she needed to halt the spread of the pathogen.

She harvested a two-inch slice, cutting the sample into six pieces. She lined up half a dozen clean Petri dishes. Each dish received different herbs or herbal combinations to try to inhibit its growth. She harvested another specimen and divided it up. She placed her samples in beakers, added herbs, and heated over the Bunsen burners.

So far none of the herbs inhibited the growth pattern. There was a last resort. She had yet to try using bark and needles from the old enchanted Hemlock tree which grew near the coven's sacred circle. She'd ask Darla tonight at the coven meeting if she could have some needles and bark. Darla was guardian of the tree, so permission was necessary.

She pulled her gloves off and dropped them in the garbage can. She turned around and there he was, Noah. He leaned casually against the door frame. She was too stunned to do anything, but stand there like one of the statues she was going to plant on the bottom of the ocean.

He came nearer; the lab seemed much, much smaller with him in it. He reached up, took her goggles off, laid them on the table. One arm around her waist, he drew her close. Smell of sea and fish permeated her nose. His free hand moved to her neck sending quivers down her spine. Drawing her close, he pressed his lips to hers, caressing her mouth more than kissing.

She slid her hands up his chest. His muscles were hard beneath her fingertips. Her senses reeled as if short circuited. He'd come back to her, he was here, he was kissing her.

He broke away first, kissing down her neck to the hollow in her throat. A heady sensation; she didn't want him to stop.

"Ella," he whispered, "we need to talk."

She tingled inside when he said her name. Yes, they should talk, now rather than later. She needed to clear up what *this* was between them. Before she could say anything, he released her and stepped back. "Evan and I talked after I left you last night. I couldn't think of anything but you all night."

He ran a hand through his hair. "I don't understand everything about you and the coven. But I want to learn. I want to be part of your life." His smile reached his eyes and he held out a hand to her. "I want to make our relationship work."

She took his hand, linking their fingers together. "Come inside. We'll have a glass of wine and I'll answer any questions you have."

He leaned in, kissed her, and sent new spirals of ecstasy through her.

Mischell! She had forgotten the mermaid. How much time until Mischell would start her change?

Ella hadn't planned on introducing them, but she didn't have a choice. "I have a surprise waiting in the house for you, Captain." She couldn't hide the giggle bubbling up.

"Noah, please call me Noah." He flashed a grin her way. "I like surprises."

"Noah, remember what you told me, how you were rescued by a pink haired mermaid?"

"Yes. I was afraid you would laugh, but you didn't. Did I thank you for that?"

She opened the door to the cottage and walked in. "Mischell, I want you to meet someone."

Mischell started to stand she looked from Ella to Noah and back again, and sat back down. She took a red Tootsie Roll Pop out of her mouth.

Noah seemed at a loss for words. He stood just inside the door, his mouth gaping open. "You're her! But how can that be?" he said, with a slow, disbelieving shake of his head.

He walked over to Mischell. "Hell, you're identical to the mermaid."

Mischell stood up. She pointed her Tootsie Roll Pop at Noah. "*I am* the mermaid who saved you. A thank you would be appropriate. I don't save just anyone who falls in the sea."

Mischell fell to the floor, her human legs replaced by an iridescent mermaid tail flopping like a fish out of water. "We've got to get her to Turtle Point. She's *changing*!" Ella cried.

Noah bent down and scooped up the teen mermaid.

"James' bag—Ella, bring my bags," Mischell mumbled, her eyes rolling back in her head.

Ella picked up James' shoe bag and another smaller bag and followed Noah to her truck. Noah lowered Mischell into the truck bed. Ella pulled a coverlet from behind the seat in the cab and tucked it around Mischell. Mischell's skin was starting to turn iridescent pink.

"The keys are in the truck. You drive fast—I'll sit in back with Mischell. Hurry, her gills are next and she won't be able to *breathe* on land."

Chapter Ten

Noah drove the old truck out onto the highway, and headed north along the coast to Turtle Point. He looked in the rearview mirror to see Ella spreading her hands above Mischell. Her lips moved—saying a spell, he supposed. Before learning her weird secret, he might have believed she was praying, not now. Was he the cause of Mischell changing back? God, he hoped not. Mischell had seemed distraught just before she collapsed.

The turn was coming up and a delivery truck was coming from the other direction. Ella pounded on the window, "Hurry!" she screamed.

"The dock would have been a hell of a lot closer," he grumbled.

He pushed on the gas and made a sharp turn after the delivery truck had passed. Ella's old truck barely missed hooking the rear bumper of the other truck.

He looked in the mirror again. Ella held Mischell's head and shoulders in her lap. The mermaid's face was ashen. Tears streamed down Ella's face. His stomach churned; he owed the mermaid his life. Now was his time to repay that debt.

He gunned the engine, sending a plume of sand and dust up behind the truck. Reaching the point, he stopped the truck, and leaped out. "Is she...?"

"Dead? No, but she's close. Her gills are changing. I called James—he'll meet us on the point."

"Who's James?"

"Not now, Noah. Help me get her to the water." Ella's mouth was set in a grim line.

This couldn't be good. He hefted Mischell in his arms and made a dash after Ella who charged down the path.

They made their way down a thirty-foot embankment to a small beach hidden by rock outcroppings. Noah stepped out into the cold surf, wondering at what point he should dunk the slight girl under the water. She was writhing and wiggling becoming difficult to hold, no doubt sensing the sea. Waves lapped his knees, edging up his thighs, pushing him back and drawing him on. Seawater now swirled around Mischell and she truly began to strain away from him. Her color was looking much better—less gray.

"Noah, next wave take her further out in the water. If you need me to help carry her I can."

"I got her, you lead the way."

"Noah, when she revives completely, you can go back to safety on shore," she said.

He looked at Ella. She had changed to a sea witch. To him at this moment she was the most beautiful, courageous woman in the entire world.

On the next incoming wave, Noah forged through waist-high water carrying the mermaid. He was five feet behind Ella when Mischell pushed away from him into the ocean, her flukes brushing his stomach as he let go. He wished he could see underwater. Ocean saltiness stung his mouth and the sea beat stinging sand against his skin.

Past the breaker line, Ella signaled him to go back. "We'll be fine. James is almost here. Wait on shore for me."

He swam hard long, strong strokes, body surfing in on waves.

Once on shore, he looked at the ocean. Ella and Mischell were further out now. They bobbed on a deep blue surface for a couple of minutes longer. Noah watched as the two swam further out. Before disappearing under water, Mischell slapped her tail, as if to say she was okay.

If there were only something he could do. He pinched the bridge of his nose, and hunkered down on a rock to wait. Who was

James? He hadn't seen a rescue boat anywhere. He shook his head at disbelief of this whole situation. He *had* been rescued by a mermaid. He *had* met said mermaid and brought her back to the ocean. His love interest was a sea witch who swam without scuba gear, and lit candles with a flick of her wrist.

Ella laughed and he glanced up to see her standing in knee deep water. She looked out to sea and waved. Beyond the crashing breakers, a long tentacle waved back and slid into the sea. Ella's clothes were dripping wet and clung to her curves. She crossed to Noah. He pulled her down on his lap.

She kissed him. Her lips were cool, and beaded with sea water. "I can't go into town looking like this. I would freak out the good people of Waxing."

"I'll get you home. Don't worry; no one will see you."

She slumped against him. "Mischell is going to be okay. James will take her to her guardians. She was breathing underwater and could swim on her own by the time I left."

"Put your arms around my neck," he ordered. "Hang on." He gathered her in his arms and climbed up the path.

Noah laid her down in the bed of the truck. He studied her eyes, they were half closed from weariness. Her metamorphous had taken its toll on her. He pulled the blanket up to her chin. Heaviness dragged at his arms and legs. He couldn't imagine how tired Ella must be.

She was shivering. "Hang on, baby," he said. Little green remained in her hair, but her skin sparkled in the sunshine. "We'll be home in five minutes."

"Home," she sighed, and closed her eyes.

# # #

Tonight was the coven meeting. Darla had requested Noah and Evan both be present. What the high witch wants the high witch gets, so Noah would be there. Actually, he had seemed anxious to attend their meeting.

Something was in the air. Darla hinted at a problem in the woods. Tightness spread across Ella's chest, as her foreboding dream resurfaced.

Ella stepped out of the shower, got dressed and dried her hair. She clipped her hair into place on top of her head. Picking up a strand of seashells she wove it through her hair. Noah was asleep on her couch. She stared down at him. He'd been through so much. Losing his boat, his friend, finding out Magick does exist and a coven of witches lives in town.

She reached down and gently slipped the chain out from under his shirt. He always wore the chain. A medallion of St. Christopher lay in her hand.

He captured her wrist in a gentle hold. "Bruce gave this medallion to me the day before he died."

"I wasn't sure what you wore on the chain, only that you always wear it." She laid the medallion on his chest. "It's time we go. The coven meeting starts in ten minutes."

Instead of getting up, he pulled her down on top of him. A current of desire rolled through her. He kissed her deeply. Her calm was shattered by the strength of passion in his kiss. Regret filled her as she forced herself to pull back. "We'll come back here after the meeting." She touched his nose with the tip of her finger. "And we'll start right where we left off, okay?"

"I'm holding you to it." He waggled his eyebrows, a devilish look in his eyes.

# # #

Noah parked the truck in front of Darla's house. He opened Ella's door, grabbed her backpack, and pulled her into his arms planting a kiss on her rose bud lips. Evan pulled up behind them, lights from his truck spotlighting their embrace. Ella waved and hooked her arm through Noah's, and gave him an encouraging squeeze. They waited on the sidewalk for Hettie and Evan

"Hey, Noah, glad you came. Good to see you." Evan clapped him on the back.

"I have to support my lady," Noah said. Nervous didn't begin to describe how he felt. He was going to attend a coven meeting. It wasn't high on his list of things to do. What the hell had he been thinking? Why Evan and he were being summoned to the meeting was a puzzle. Witches, Magick and the entire hoodoo, surrounding the Coven was hard to comprehend, even though he had seen Magick first hand. Witnessing Magick, didn't make Magick any easier to accept as true.

He'd made a promise to see Ella's world, like it or not he'd go to the meeting. Leaves of a stately American elm growing in Darla's front yard, rustled from the evening breeze. Unsure if it was nerves or light wind, Noah shivered like the leaves overhead.

The small group walked in unison up the wide brick walkway. Ella rapped on the red front door. Noah suppressed a growing coldness in his stomach.

Darla opened the door. She wore a red caftan edged in silver brocade, and a matching brocade headband that was having a hard time holding back her black unruly hair. The warm glow from candles spilled onto the porch. Incense flowed out and around them, enticing and soothing. "Ah-h, you boys will have to wait on the bench." She pointed toward the end of the porch where purple twinkle lights coiled around the bannister and shone on a wooden bench and ivy covered trellis. "You may come in when our business is concluded."

Ella and Hettie disappeared inside.

"We've been benched like a couple of school boys." Noah stuffed his hands in his pockets and ambled down to the bench.

"Hey, I've never been privileged to attend a meeting." Evan said, "Something's different tonight." He sat down on the bench, his arms resting on his knees and hands dangling between his legs. "This will be a first for me, too."

Noah wondered if he could really fit into Ella's world. The answer lay behind the red door that much he was certain of.

THE WITCH WITH THE TRIDENT TATTOO

Chapter Eleven

Once inside, Ella headed for the guest room the coven sometimes used to change their clothes. Hettie followed.

Ella slipped into her silk azure caftan and placed a headband of seashells on her head.

Hettie slipped her charcoal gray caftan over her head and tugged it down over her expanding belly. "Won't be long until the baby will be too big and I won't fit in my regular clothes. I guess that calls for a shopping trip."

Ella smiled at her friend. "You name the day, I'm up for a shopping trip!"

They entered Darla's family room designated for coven meetings. Ella sat down on a couch next to Mia Deforest, the elder of their group. Mia smoothed down her mahogany brown caftan. Mia's twisted ash spirit staff leaned against her leg.

"How are you, dear?" Mia said a twinkle in her hazel eyes. "I understand you've bonded with Noah."

My, how quickly news traveled. "Yes," Ella said, as heat rose up her neck.

"And what about your project, the one you're working on for Poseidon?"

"The remedy for reversing RTB-1? Hard, a real struggle trying to find a solution, there's been several setbacks." Ella, nervous, picked imaginary fuzz off her dress.

"Perhaps, you are looking for a cure when you should be looking for the source?" Mia caressed her staff.

"Thanks for the advice. I hope to get some answers tonight."

On an aromatic swirl of essence of mint, Ivy Larsdatter entered the room twirling to show off her new green caftan, a rope of gold cord encircled her slender waist. She was the youngest at twenty years and still learning the Craft. "I've started taking an herbal class at Middlesex community college." Her enthusiasm sparkled across her face. "Next semester I'm taking a botany class. I plan to grow my own herbs in a greenhouse by the time I graduate."

"That's marvelous," Mia enthused.

Darla seemed to float into the meeting room. She carried all necessary items for casting a circle. She handed a broom to a surprised Ivy. "Sweep the sacred space of negative energy, young one."

"Me? I've never been called on before." Ivy said as she took the broom.

"Look lively. You're being called on now."

After Ivy completed her task, Darla picked up a bowl of water and added a pinch of salt from a crystal salt cellar sitting on the end table. She stirred the water clockwise and next sprinkled water around the edge to cleanse and consecrate the circle.

Darla waved a hand toward the door and it opened to reveal a startled Rosalba with her fist raised to knock. "Tardy as usual, come in, come in." Darla said, allowing a little annoyance to seep into her tone. "You almost missed circle time."

Rosalba swept in surrounded by an aura of distain. "Sorry, I was held up because Leah wanted me to bring a message to the circle."

Darla rolled her eyes. "Go change, so we can begin our meeting."

"Change? I'm ready!" Instead of the usual attire of a caftan she had opted for an olive green tunic adorned with a large rainbow colored peace sign over black leggings.

"Fine, let us begin, Ella seal the circle so the quarters can be called." Darla dictated.

Ella stood in the center of the cleansed circle, pointed her wand to the elemental gateway of earth. Meanwhile the coven chanted in unison.

Why are Darla and Rosalba at odds? Ella wondered. There was definite friction between them. Energy in the room felt off, because of their negativity.

"We must protect our hemlock tree. This tree is critical to our Magick and our connection to the past. Ella is dealing with an important problem too, but it is Ella's problem to fix." Darla turned around inside the circle. She looked each one of the witches in the eye. She pointed at Mia, the crone. "I want you to lead a quest of three. Hettie, you came through the hemlock portal, Mia, you are a witch of the forest and every animal, plant, and tree is in your care, so you two and...Ivy."

"Me?" Ivy smiled.

"Yes. You, by your own words, are studying botanicals at college. I feel you'll be a good addition to this quest."

Ella started to raise her hand, but lowered it as Darla continued.

"Here's what we know:

One-environmentalists saved the tree from lumber mills.

Two-the tree is a portal.

Three-leaves and bark are falling off our tree in the wrong season.

Four-the Magick of ages are stored in that tree." Darla stopped. She turned, looked directly at Rosalba. "And your spirit guide, Leah, did she tell you anything? Is that why you were late?"

Rosalba brought her hands in front of her in prayer form, bent forward in a bow of respect toward Darla. "Yes. She said the tree is in great danger. Black Magick from the past is trying to come through. To save our tree, we have to release the wizard who resides inside."

"Release the wizard? And what of our Magick? He's the one who protects it." Darla whispered. Fear had crept into her eyes, and fear raised her dark locks so they floated about her head. She looked like Medusa.

Rosabla took a step back. "First thing we have to release the wizard. He will help us to save the tree, and the Hemlock will recover."

The meeting was coming to a close when Ella finally raised her hand.

"Ella, do you have something to add?" Darla nodded in her direction.

"No, I think we've covered everything. But I do have a new request. You told us our Hemlock tree is in danger, and I know the tree is a source of Magick in the woodlands. Still, I am requesting a few green twigs, perhaps some leaves attached and a piece of bark. Magick held in the tree may be an antidote for the unknown pathogen, RTB-1, growing in the ocean."

Darla's eyes turned a shade darker brown. Ella's mouth went dry. She realized how much the Hemlock tree meant to Darla, and the whole coven.

"The tree is suffering. I'm not so sure taking a piece of his living tissue when he is in a weaken state would be good. Help yourself to anything that's fallen off the tree on to the ground." She looked pointedly at Ella. "But your problem is in the ocean. Your solution is also in the ocean. You've learned to trust Noah, and he trusts you. Together you can solve this crisis, in the sea."

"But…" Ella stammered.

"No buts! My focus is to save the tree. He and the Wizard residing in him are our connection to the past, present and future. We must not fail the tree or the wizard. I am doing everything in my power to save them both."

The witches stood, touching hands. They leaned over in unison and flung their heads back to look at the ceiling while they chanted.

"Bless this coven, and guide Ella on her quest,
Let the puzzle of the tree be solved,
Let our knowledge rise up.
Guide our men as they join in.
To all things on earth, blessed be, blessed be."

"You may ask Evan and Noah to join us now, Hettie," Darla said.

A chill passed over Ella. Both Poseidon and Darla had thrown the ocean problem back in her lap. At the current growth rate, she had a matter of days to figure out a key to unlock the answer, before the pathogen reached the shore.

Noah followed her in and sat down beside her on the loveseat. He put his arm across her shoulders.

"Welcome, Noah and Evan. You must swear to keep our coven and Magick secret." Darla stood in the middle of the room and in her hands she held her sacred knife and Grimoire, the book of spells. "Come," she waved the two men forward. "Place your left hand on the Grimoire, Noah. You also, Evan, perfect. The ceremony tonight is to induct you into our coven. You will be guardians of our secrets. I'm going to nick your fingers and put three drops of blood from each of you on the Grimoire."

She picked up her sacred knife and pricked their fingers one at a time. Noah sucked in his breath as the ceremonial knife pricked his finger.

"Perfect," Darla said, and squeezed drops of blood from each of their fingers. Red droplets landed on the Grimoire and blended together.

An unnatural stillness enveloped Noah as he watched their blood droplets sizzle on the book of Magick, until the blood evaporated in a whiff of smoke.

"Didn't take long, did it? If you ever betray us we will find you. Ella, get these gentlemen band-aids."

# # #

Once they were in the truck heading home, Noah reached over and squeezed her arm. "Evan and I were discussing how to explore Razor Trench. You said you can only stay underwater for a couple of hours. What if Evan, you and I go out in my boat, and we'll dive together?"

"What?"

"Don't you see we'd have two sets of eyes looking for the throat of the underwater cave? I can scuba dive—I was in the SEALS for five years. I'll follow you down to the trench and we can look together for a cave or another way in." He glanced over with a wide grin. "Evan will man our boat, be our safety person, and I'll be your backup."

"I have backup when I dive." She wasn't going to have Noah in danger. Not after she'd found him, her mate.

He hit his hand on the steering wheel. "Damn, Ella, you're not going alone."

"I told you I won't be alone, I'll have James."

"Okay, I'll bite, who the hell is James?" He turned the truck into the drive and parked and faced her. "We've been dancing around this question for a while. Well, who is he?"

"He's my familiar." Ella opened the truck door and got out.

He caught her as she put her key in the front entry lock of the cottage. He placed his hand over hers. Her heart melted; for a moment she couldn't speak. She turned the key and led the way inside.

He grasped her shoulder and turned her around. His jaw set in a ridged line. "So who's James?"

"James is an Atlantic octopus." She smiled.

"Octopus?" His eyebrows shot up. "You're kidding me!"

"No, Yes, I mean no I'm not kidding, and yes he is an octopus. We communicate telepathically. When he's close, we can communicate. By close I mean around ten miles away or so." She sighed. "Would you like to meet him?"

"Uh, maybe some time," he said, looking green around the edges. "There's no doubt Octopi are smart, but I had no idea they could speak mentally or otherwise."

Would the Magick realm be too much for the captain? She hoped that Noah would come around to accepting all things Magical. If they were to share a life together, he needed to be fully on board with his belief in and protection of the Coven, Magick and James.

His deep chocolate eyes pinned her, and she could not turn away. "Can we table our talk till morning?"

"Sure." She stepped closer to him and placed her palm on his chest. "Shall we finish what we started earlier, before the meeting?"

His eyes lit up, he pulled her close and took her mouth with his. He pressed her back against the wall. His hands swept down her hips, back up to her waist starting a fire in her belly.

She knew she wanted him, but the depth of that want wasn't clear till now. A shiver shimmied up her spine as he removed her seashell headband and hair clips. He undid the tie of the azure caftan she wore. Silk slipped down to puddle on the floor.

She pulled away from his kiss long enough to whisper, "The bedroom".

He gathered her up in his arms and carried her in, laid her on the bed. "You are so beautiful, my little witch." With a sheepish grin on his face he proceeded to disrobe.

Ella reached out and took his hand and drew him down to her.

On a low purr, she ran her hands over his shoulders. Hard muscles, strong muscles all hers to explore and love. "Very nice," she murmured and brushed her lips over his.

Winding her hair around his hand he brought her lips to his in a crushing, scorching kiss. With her breasts against his chest she could feel his rapid heartbeat. She wrapped her bare leg around him and pulled him even closer. He was hard for her.

There was no going back. Ella wanted Noah, all of him. He slid his hand up and down her bare thigh feeding the passion within her.

They made love, touching, exploring, again and again. He gave her pleasure after pleasure, sweeping her away on a tide of desire until she thought she'd die without him inside her.

Skin slick with desire, he drove inside of her. She gripped his hands and surrendered to the movement, the moment. She cried out, embracing the glorious rollercoaster ride. Up, up and up towards the heavens and free falling back down. Her world exploded.

She lay in the tangled sheets too exhausted to move. Noah lay on his back eyes shut, his chest heaving from their lovely marathon of lovemaking.

She liked feeling his heart racing under her hand, knowing she'd made that happen.

"Well, captain, now what?"

He laughed, rolled onto his side, hooked an arm around her and turned her to face him. "I'm starving. Famished, how about you?"

"No problem. I can whip up some eggs and toast. And there might be some leftover blueberry pie. Would that do?" She began to untangle herself from the sheets.

"Wait. It's not food I'm after. You look like a goddess all gift wrapped in those sheets." Between each word, he planted kisses on her shoulder, neck, and face. "I want to be the one to unwrap you."

"Oh." A delicious shudder heated her body.

Chapter Twelve

Noah made fried eggs, bacon and toast. After he set the table, he poured coffee into mugs. When he looked up Ella stood in the doorway. "Good morning, sunshine." He handed her a steaming mug. Her unruly fairy blonde hair hung to her waist, her cheeks rosy from a night of love making.

"Thanks." She looked over the top of the mug and took a sip.

He moved closer to her, kissed her cheek. "You look lovely this morning. Sit, we'll finish our discussion now."

She sat, running her fingers through her messy hair. His groin tightened as he remembered removing the clips from her hair, and the way her waist long hair had tumbled down her bare back.

He put their breakfast on plates and sat down across from her. "I called Evan and told him to top off the gas tank and get the Mystic Mermaid ready. If you are up to going out today, we'll head over to the docks in say half an hour?"

"Noah, I think it's good of you to take me out to the coordinates for Razor Trench. However," she pointed her fork at him, "you've got to promise me you'll stay aboard till I have time to check out the cave."

"Yeah, yeah." Like hell he would. He wasn't going to risk her going by herself, and only an octopus for protection? "Let's talk this over with Evan on our way out. We'll come up with a plan of action, I promise."

"I want you to meet James. You won't be able to talk to him, but he is intelligent, and when he knows you're my friend, he will watch out for you too." She smiled and tilted her head to the side.

A freaking octopus! She wanted him to meet the thing? He wasn't sure he'd be up for it... But to appease her, he would meet *James*. "Okay, I'll meet him," he said grudgingly.

# # #

Noah watched in fascination as Ella began to morph into a sea witch. She wore an oversized white peasant shirt, mid-thigh in length. Her trident tattoo showed on her right calf. Starting at her feet and moving up her legs were iridescent green sparkles. Her hands and face were beginning to change too.

Evan cut the engine and dropped anchor.

"What's the depth here?" Noah hollered.

"The gauge is showing sixteen fathoms."

"James is here. I'm going in and talk him into meeting you." She laid a green glittery hand on Noah's arm and kissed him on the cheek. "I'll apprise him of the plan."

Noah chuckled.

"What's so funny?"

"I was thinking of vegetables, the Jolly Green Giant in particular." He chuckled again. "I have my own green goddess." Pretty, the hint of blush he observed right before she dove over the side. He had checked his oxygen tank, buoyancy compensator, dive computer and the rest of his diving gear before leaving the dock this morning.

Evan, being an experienced diver too, helped him recheck everything. Noah donned his wetsuit and flippers.

Ella surfaced nearby. "Captain, I want you to meet James." His green goddess sat on a large tentacle of a very large octopus. The boat and octopus bobbed on a glossy surface of gently undulating waves.

Noah swallowed hard. He couldn't believe what he was seeing.

"Holy shit, is that what I think it is?" Evan's mouth hung open in disbelief.

"Yep, my lady's pet octopus." Noah reached a hand over the side and one of the beast's tentacles wrapped around his arm and pulled him into the sea.

"Noah!" Evan yelled.

Noah sat perched on an outstretched tentacle next to Ella. "It's okay. James is Ella's familiar." He couldn't believe how gentle this twelve-foot octopus was. He trusted Ella, and Ella trusted the octopus.

"Okay, now you get back in the boat and wait for us." Ella smiled, cupped his cheek in her hand and planted a passionate kiss on his lips. She pushed him off the tentacle. He swam to the rope ladder and climbed onto the boat. He looked around for Ella and James but they had vanished beneath the calm surface, leaving only a ripple behind.

"I wouldn't have believed there was a friendly octopus in the ocean, except I saw one with my own eyes." Evan said, scratching his chin. "Hard to believe, hard to believe." He pulled up the ladder.

Ten, fifteen and finally twenty minutes went by. Noah stood looking at where the ocean had swallowed Ella and James. "I'm going in. Their dive is taking too long; they should've been back by now." He reached for his equipment.

"Noah," Ella's voice reached him. "We found a tunnel. James can go in but he won't have much room to maneuver—it opens into an air chamber and he wouldn't be able to breathe or move around well out of the water."

"I'm coming."

"No! I'll go down first. If I discover anything worth exploring further, I'll come back and get you, just like we planned on the way out. No use using up your air tank if there's nothing to explore." She did a backward dive and disappeared underwater.

Plan or not, he was stunned to be left behind, Noah strapped on his weight belt. He made sure his tool belt included a knife, rope and two flashlights. Evan helped Noah with his tank, and rest of his equipment. He was ready in five minutes and sat on the rail waiting.

After twenty minutes, he could wait no longer. "We should be back in half an hour. If not, something has gone terribly wrong." Noah adjusted his mask, put the regulator in his mouth and slipped into the ocean.

He searched down through dark blue depths for a sign of Ella or the giant octopus; not seeing either one of them, he swam toward Razor Trench which bordered Razor Island. Soon, his gauges showed a depth of ninety feet. He had only been under a few minutes yet a chill took hold of him. Water dark with minute debris which floated thick as sand in an hourglass, this was not what he had expected to encounter. He emerged from a thick murky band of debris to find the narrow trench roughly one fathom down.

He checked his buoyancy compensator and made an adjustment. His dive computer showed he had plenty of air left. The percolating sound of his bubbles as they made their way toward the surface, reminded him of his coffee pot, and boy, what he'd give for a strong cup of Joe right now.

He surveyed the ocean floor. Murky bubbles rose from carnage resting on the bottom. Each bubble filled with rotting flora and fauna, scattering lifeless shells and skeletons of death as they burst. Ella had said there was carnage everywhere; plumes of brown and black kelp waved like flags of death. Small marine life lay motionless, where crabs should have been scurrying around. His heart pounded hard in his chest.

He slowed his breathing down, couldn't afford to waste oxygen. Calmer, he swam to the edge of the narrow trench. No way could he get down there, too constricted. He noticed a pinprick of a light at the far end, where the trench merged into the rock precipice. The light didn't seem to be electrical but more like a reflection of sunlight?

He kicked his flippers, swimming to the end of the trench. When he reached the rock wall rising halfway to the surface, he continued to explore along the rocky edifice looking for an opening. A sudden unexpected current caught him and swept him around the rock outcropping, banging him up against a ledge. After stabilizing himself in a nook, he proceeded to check his dive computer and gauges. Time meant air usage; he must be conservative with his oxygen. Everything was in order. The current had been strong and was gone in a matter of seconds. Odd, that.

He shined his flashlight into the far reaches of the recess to discover the stone throat of an underwater cave. He drifted for a few seconds suspended in the sea, before going in. A current surged through the tunnel, bashing him against the uneven side, wrenching his arm and sending his flashlight crashing into the side before winking out. There could be no darkness dense as an underwater cave.

Something moved past him in the darkness brushing his leg. His heart beat like a drummer on steroids. He swallowed, nervous now. He remembered his other flashlight; he groped in the oppressive darkness until he found the torch, unfastened it from his belt, turned it on. He touched the sides along the tunnel wall. Sharp with outcroppings of rock, the tunnel curved to the left and soon he was headed up through the entry tunnel. Around a corner, a light shone down into the water from an air-locked cavern.

He bobbed his head up out of the dark water, turned off his regulator to listen. He could hear voices echoing in the distance, but couldn't make out what they were saying. The cavern was probably eight fathoms from the surface inside the bowels of Razor Island. Somehow, someway there was breathable air inside.

He'd go back to his boat and tell Evan what he'd found. Change tanks and come back. With the next surge of water, a long tentacle pushed him up on the sandy floor of the cavern.

The tentacle patted Noah on his leg. The bulbous octopus head popped up out of the water. *James!* His pupils widened and narrowed as if trying to communicate something to Noah; the tentacle kept pointing toward the interior of the cavern. *Ella! She must be in there. That had to be the reason James was pointing to the interior.*

Noah gave a thumb up, universal language for 'okay'.

Noah shrugged out of his tank and dropped his weight belt on the sand He was in the middle of removing his BC vest when a bright pink head of hair bobbed up beside the giant octopus. "Took you long enough to find us," Mischell sputtered. "James said Kenn has Ella tied up. She's starting to change to her human form. There's no time to waste, you need to save her now!"

Who was Kenn? He threw off his flippers and grabbed his knife. The woman had too many secrets for her own good. Crouched low, he made his way following the sound of raised voices.

"Kenn, you need to stop destroying the ocean. There's no point in creating all the devastation," Ella pleaded.

"You *don't* know what I've been through, sea witch! I've never had respect. My father banished me from Atlantis with only the clothes on my back, and nothing else, because you *tattled!*" The man snarled. "While you are given a whole coastline to command," he spit out.

"I am a caretaker, I don't command anything. What you've done to the sea here is horrendous," she said, choking on her words. "Do you really think this will get you the attention you crave from your *father?*"

"Ah-h, but all blame will rest squarely on your shoulders, my dear." The metallic sound of a blade being drawn from a sheath reverberated through the cavern. "And you won't be around to tell the truth. It'll be an open and shut case. I'll simply beseech my father for a chance to redeem myself by curing *your* plague which is invading the ecosystem. And since I've almost created the cure, I'll come out a hero."

"You're wrong." The high pitch of desperation in her voice had Noah dragging his hand down his face.

"My experiments will prove I've been trying to find a cure. There are many people who know I've been working on a cure. You can't kill them all."

This had gone on long enough, Noah waited, watching for his chance. Ella's hands were bound and she sat on the gritty sand floor. The cavern was big enough to hold a two-story house.

The tall thin man had an auburn beard and shoulder length stringy hair. His noticeable limp gave him a lopsided gait. He wore a shabby medieval styled jacket that hung with a flare well below his hips. Ragged jeans and black fringed boots were the icing on the cake. This creep had been living here. The asymmetrical cavern held a bed, table, chairs, and a small lab table. Sitting on top was a microscope, beakers and an industrial light hanging high above. Wires ran along the top of the cavern and out a tunnel west toward what Noah thought must be the interior of Razor Island.

Noah heard the distant rumble of a generator. Probably somewhere in the tunnel, would be his guess.

He was blind with fury at Kenn for terrorizing her, but he held himself steady, looking for a chance to tackle the guy that wouldn't endanger Ella. Kenn paced back and forth in front of Ella, slapping the flat side of an ancient-looking sword against his palm.

"What to do, what to do?" Kenn sneered.

Mischell crept up behind Noah and tapped him on the shoulder. He jumped. "What are you doing on land?" he whispered.

"I'll go distract Kenn. Maybe you can jump him?" Mischell said her voice tinged with excitement.

"You know that piece of shit?"

"He's Poseidon's bastard son. He has been evil since the day he was born. I overheard the other mermaids say he threatened them too. But they swam away to the north." She wiggled her sequined bustier up, patted down her skirt, and marched out of the shadows before Noah could stop her.

Ella saw Mischell first and shook her head no.

Alerted, Kenn turned, brandishing the sword. "And what are you doing here?"

"I got lost. You know me, Kenn, I'm always in the wrong place at the wrong time," Mischell said.

"Oh, yeah, the little kleptomaniac," he spit out. "You're a long way from your pod. They keep to the shore, don't they? What are the guardians going to say?"

She walked past Kenn and he turned to keep her in view. Noah took his opening and ran on silent feet, reaching Kenn, wrestling him to the floor and sending the sword flying.

Ella screamed, "No!"

The men rolled around each other, each trying for the first blow. Kenn landed a punch and stars danced across Noah's vision. Sand flew up from the floor, kicked there by boots. Kenn fought hard for such a thin, sinewy, nasty piece of work. Kenn shoved both his feet against Noah's stomach, sending him flying ten feet. He landed on his back, the air knocked out. He could hardly breathe.

The prick of a sword against his throat brought his attention back to the crazed man standing over him. "Who might you be?" Kenn said, between heavy breaths. His mouth took on an unpleasant twist. He wiped a hand across his bleeding lip.

Noah swiped the blade away and rolled to his feet, his knife once again in his hand. "I'm the man who's going to kick your sorry ass."

Kenn raised his sword high overhead and charged. They met, and with a quick maneuver, Noah disarmed him and held his knife to Kenn's throat. "One word from you, Ella, and he's no longer in the land of the living."

"No more killing. I'll send James for Poseidon. He will want to know and…" she trailed off, and slumped to the floor.

Noah kicked Kenn's sword toward the water, satisfied when the blade splashed into the water. He pushed Kenn to the ground. "Stay here. Or move and give me the chance I want to slice you up for bait."

He knelt by Ella. Mischell had untied her hands and Ella lay so still. Her time had run out and she had completed her change, her underwater abilities gone.

"Watch out," Mischell cried.

Noah turned to see Kenn charging again, holding a large iron pot as a weapon. Before Noah could stand up, a long tentacle reached out and yanked Kenn off his feet. The tentacle pulled him toward the water. Kenn screamed all the way till the tentacle submerged him. Another tentacle emerged from the water, waving the sword overhead.

With the cavern no longer protected by Kenn's Magick, the incoming tide pushed a surge of water over the lip of stone at the entrance, flooding the floor and growing deeper by the moment. Noah made lightning-fast calculations.

"Mischell, can you talk to James?"

"Yeah, sure, why?" She wrinkled her forehead.

"I need to give you both instructions on how to use my regulator and oxygen tank. We need to get Ella to safety on the boat." He quickly outlined stop points for rising safely to the surface and how to read the depth gauge.

"Right got it, what about you?"

"I love her. She's weak after changing and she needs to get to land. Ella won't survive when this cavern floods."

"You won't either. What happens to you?" Tears filled the mermaid's eyes.

"I'll wait here. James can bring my spare tank. Go on now. Talk to James, make sure he understands how important the decompression times are." Frustrated, he held Ella in his arms, kissing her face and the top of her head. Hugging her tight to his chest, wishing she could make the change more than once a day.

"Noah, I love you. You need to go back," she whispered, "not me."

"Captain's orders, you're going back to the Mystic Mermaid and safety." He swallowed a lump in his throat, knowing he could well die here in this cave. "I'm going to give you instructions on how to breathe using the regulator. James knows about decompression—he'll get you to safety."

Wading through knee deep water, he carried her to the ledge above the sea tunnel. James wrapped his tentacle around her, cradling her. Noah attached the tank and mask to Ella and put the regulator in her mouth. He told her what to expect, and what to do. How much she would remember in her state he didn't know. With blurred vision, he suppressed a sob. He had found his love and now might well lose her.

Submerged right below the surface, James held Ella; she was breathing in and out through the regulator like a pro. They sunk from view. The next surge of water knocked him down and pushed him across the floor; he bumped into Mischell. "When can you change back?" He was suddenly fearful for the young girl's life.

"I'm staying here. I have time yet and I can change back when I want to. But if I'm too long on land, I'll change with no warning." She smiled. "I have an expiration time limit."

They climbed up the rock wall till they could go no further, and sat on a narrow ledge, waiting. The ocean surged and retreated, each upsurge pushed the water closer to where they sat.

"Was Kenn living here?" Noah asked.

"No, he created this room, making a trap. He wanted to kill Ella."

The next surge of the sea flooded the tunnel where the generator sat, and it sputtered out. In a blink the light disappeared. Noah closed his eyes against the darkness surrounding them. He was going to die, drowned like a rat in a sewer. "Mischell, can you see in the dark?"

"A little, I can make out shapes."

He flicked on his underwater flashlight. "This should help till James gets back." If the octopus returned in time, he didn't even want to go there. James had to make it back in time.

"Your friend is okay," she said.

"My friend?"

"The one who went down with your boat the day I rescued you." She smoothed down her skirt. "You see, I couldn't rescue both of you. I wish I could have. I'm not supposed to rescue anyone and because I did, I got in big trouble, and ran away. You don't need to worry—he didn't end up in Davey Jones' Locker. Guardians took him, my guardians." She patted her chest.

"He's not dead?" He couldn't believe what he was hearing. Bruce alive? Impossible, he'd watched Bruce drift away and sink.

"He's not dead, but he's not exactly human either."

"Well, what the hell is he?" He fought nausea bubbling up inside. James had had plenty of time to reach the boat and come back. Where was he?

"I guess you'd call him a merman. In a few years, his change will be complete. He is living a good life. Anna Bell, she claimed him as her mate." She patted Noah on the arm.

"I won't leave you, but I'm going to change now." She slipped into the salty sea water pooling around their feet.

In the beam from his flashlight, Mischell looked like a hallucination. Pink spiked hair, blue sequined bustier and iridescent fish tail a full blown mermaid.

The next surge of water pushed them closer to the ceiling; he could touch it now. He clenched his jaw. One more wave and he would be picking pieces of the ceiling rocks out of his teeth.

"James is here," she shouted.

A tentacle wrapped around his leg, steadying him. Three tentacles held his equipment. Noah grabbed the tank strapped it to his back, next he put the mask, and regulator on. Here goes nothing, he thought, and gave James a thumbs-up. Another tentacle wrapped around his arm and pulled him into the flooded cavern and towards the exit.

Noah aimed his light back through black water, to see Mischell swimming after them. He swore he'd never forget today. He didn't know if Ella was okay or not. She had definitely made it back to his boat, but in what condition?

# # #

Noah's ride back to the *Mystic Mermaid* with James and Mischell was surreal. James lifted him on to the boat. "Bye, Noah." Mischell bobbed in the ocean next to the half-submerged octopus. "Tell lla I love her."

"I will." Crazy as it seemed, he felt he owed a thank you to the octopus. "Hey, James?" The octopus waved a long tentacle in the air. "Thanks, man, I owe you."

James waved and sunk into the depths of the ocean. Mischell slapped her tail and disappeared too.

Noah began removing his gear. "Evan! Is Ella alright?"

"Roger that. She's in your bunk." Evan yelled from the wheelhouse.

"Let's head to shore! I want solid terra firma under me."

Evan shifted the vessel into gear and pushed to full throttle.

The rumble of the engine was music to Noah's ears. His ordeal was over. Ella was safe. He climbed down into the cabin. "Hey," he said, while his heart beat a staccato in his chest.

"Hey, yourself, Captain," Ella murmured, her eyes were closed and a slip of a smile graced her lips.

He bent over and kissed her. A few sparkly green scales remained on her arms and face, her change was almost complete.

"Mischell?" Ella reached up and cupped his cheek.

He leaned into her hand. "Mischell changed before the cave flooded. She's fine." He kissed her palm. "She sends her love."

Chapter Thirteen

Two days later Ella was finally strong enough to go back to work on a cure for the malady that plagued her beloved ocean. Yesterday Noah had helped her gather new fallen leaves and twigs from inside the sacred circle surrounding the Hemlock tree. They were careful to choose only leaves and twigs still green, the color indicated there was Magick still infused in the material.

She unlocked her Magical cabinet and took out her charmed three-legged mortar and pestle. Placing them on the pristine lab table, she took down the hand held grain grinder with sharp blades which would work nicely on the twigs she and Noah had gathered.

Hope dwelled in her heart. These gifts from the Sacred Tree contained potent Magick. By combining these ingredients with the confiscated tube of serum Mischell had managed to bring back from Kenn's lab, she might be able to create an antidote for Kenn's Magical poison, the one he had used to taint the ocean.

She ground and crushed hemlock leaves in her mortar with a vigor born of desperation and carefully poured the results into a dry beaker. Adding a cup of distilled water she stirred the mixture clockwise six times, and then counter-clockwise six times. Next, she took hemlock twigs still green and inserted them in the grinder. Holding her grinder over the beaker she said a spell to extract Magick, as she turned the handle and watched twig bits fall into the beaker.

"Green leaves of Hemlock,
And mighty twigs of Hemlock,
I know you hold Magick.
Release your power to save the sea,
For this you've been handpicked

So mote it be!"

Ella set her grinder down and picked up a stirring rod. Gently she stirred her Magick potion, a foundation to start with.

"Round, round and round the sea you'll go,

To bind your Magick three drops of wax from this enchanted candlestick.

So mote it be!"

She held a binding candle over the beaker, continuing to stir whilst three drops of wax fell into a bubbling mixture. A ball of Magical energy began to form. Glimmering and shimmering as light began emanating from inside the orb. Using a watch glass for a lid, she set it on top of the beaker.

Removing Kenn's vial from her fridge she used a dropper pipet to extract a few drops of thick yellow liquid. The energy orb continued to twirl and glow inside the beaker. She removed the lid and released two more drops onto the shimmering ball.

Her stomach rolled. She was sure of her calculations, but the energy emitted from the orb was not enough to reverse Kenn's toxic malady. After adding a couple more drops with no results, her breath hitched. Kenn's cure wasn't working. If she added too much of his serum the potion would increase, instead of reverse the toxin. Now what?

She needed a catalyst. What kind? Kenn's serum was yellow, so the element needed could be sunshine or heat. She set the test tube over the Bunsen burner to warm up.

With a thermometer in the test tube to track the heat level, she watched as the temperature slowly rose. At forty degrees the serum began slowly moving, thinning out. At fifty-one degrees, the ocean temperature in late spring, the liquid swirled and danced and bubbled up in the test tube.

She removed the lid from the beaker and squeezed four more warm drops onto the Magical ball. The orb started flashing blue, yellow and green. She added more serum. A ball of energy bounced around inside the beaker exhibiting more energy than before. Flashing colors emitted from the orb merged to an aqua blue. Kenn's cure had worked once the orb had reached the same temperature as the ocean.

She didn't take her eyes off the Magical ball. She hit Noah's speed dial on her cell.

"Hello?" he said, followed by a yawn.

"It worked! The Magick worked. We did it. Kenn's cure mixed with Magick from the Hemlock quashes the life right out of RTB-1 in my lab. Can you take me out to Razor Trench? I need to test this remedy in the devastated area. We've got to stop RTB-1's growth."

"Ella that is fantastic. I'll be right there. Do you have something safe to carry the cure in?"

"Yes. I'll be ready. I love you."

"Love you too. Ella," he said, raw emotion adding a husky tone to his voice.

# # #

Noah pulled into her driveway at Shell Cottage in less than five minutes. With a square, small black case clutched to her chest, Ella stood on the porch waiting for him. He reached over and opened the truck door. She put the case on the seat and slid inside.

The *Mystic Mermaid* plowed through cold Atlantic water toward their destination. Ella stationed herself in the bow, the breeze blew her long blonde hair behind her, and Noah found his heart felt lighter than it had in a long time. When he spotted Razor Island he pulled back on the throttle and put the engine in idle.

The boat rose up and down on gentle swells as he climbed onto the deck. "Is this the right spot, Ella?" Sun beat down on the Mystic Mermaid warming him through, and he shrugged out of his jacket.

"Yes. Let me get the serum and Magick orb." She went into the cabin and brought back her square case, sitting it on the bait box she opened the case up to use for a work station. She took out

Kenn's test tube from the insulated chamber inside the case and secured it upright using an elastic loop attached to the inside edge of her case. Carefully she removed the secure lid from a receptacle which now held her Magick ball of Hemlock leaves and twigs.

"Are you ready?" Ella looked at him her sea green eyes questioning.

"Yep. What do you want me to do?"

She grinned at him. "Step back and enjoy the show." Ella walked to the side of the boat. Holding her container over the ocean so not to get any on the boat, she poured the entire warm contents into the beaker. Securing the lid back in place they watched the contents began to react. Sparks flew against the sides of the glass container. The orb bounced around inside, spinning till all the serum was absorbed. Once the ball settled down to a slower spin at the bottom of the container and began to pulse a turquoise green light, she knew it was ready.

"I'm not sure what's going to happen when this concoction comes in contact with the sea. In the controlled environment of the lab it worked." Ella removed the lid and the ball continued to spin while it rose about half way up inside the container. Slowly she turned her beaker over till the Magical orb rolled out and dropped into the ocean. Ella stared into the depths as she searched for a sign.

Noah took the beaker and test tube from her and secured them in her case. He put his arm around her shoulders and pulled her close, prepared to stand watch for however long it took to work.

After a few minutes, Ella's forehead wrinkled. "I don't understand the Magick ball should have reached Razor trench by now."

All of a sudden there was a brilliant flash of turquoise light deep underwater. Noah watched as color spread in all directions. The *Mystic Mermaid* shifted in the water, and a rumble passed through his vessel. "Is that the …"

"Yes! Magick! It worked!" Ella threw her arms around his neck. "Let's go home, Captain."

Chapter Fourteen

The next day Ella and James arrived at Poseidon's silver-gourd shaped submersible at the appointed time. She slid off the octopus's tentacle, landing on the ocean floor and stirring up a small cloud of sand sending small crustaceans scurrying off to seek shelter.

Thanks for the ride, James. I shouldn't be long. She gave his tentacle a pat.

No worries, I'll hang out by that cluster of rocks. James pointed to a hodgepodge of rocks thirty feet from Poseidon's submersible.

As James pushed off toward the rocks, Ella entered the vessel and swam up through the moon pool. She dried off using the soft towel left in the dressing room. A lovely gown hung on a brass hook. She took it down and slipped it over her head. She ran her hand over the fabric of the luxurious long aqua dress, so soft. Poseidon was treating her like a princess; this long dress was much more elegant than the robe he'd given her last time.

She was not entirely sure what to expect from him.

At her approach mermen stationed by massive doors bowed and opened the gateway to Poseidon's royal chamber. She squared her shoulders and entered. Poseidon faced one of many triangular portholes lining the wall. His dreadlocks hung down his bare back like so many snakes, writhing as he turned.

"Witch," he said, "I owe you *thanks* on behalf of my underwater kingdom. Kenn always did know how to vex me, seems he never outgrew his penchant for trouble."

Poseidon's monotone sent a shiver through Ella, much worse than if he had yelled and screamed. "What's to become of Kenn?" she inquired.

"Kenn will be brought before the Court of Trepidation. I imagine a curse of some kind will be put upon him." He raised his hand as if shooing away a fly. "Kenn will never bother you again or enter the ocean in your jurisdiction."

Ella was almost sorry for Kenn. *Almost*. Judges who sat on this court panel were not known for compassion. Her friend, James, her familiar, had only stolen a pair of sandals and he was cursed to live his life as an octopus till the courts deemed he'd learned his lesson. Of course, the sandals had belonged to Poseidon. At least the shoes James now collected were lost ones. Nearly emotionally drained she was ready to be on her way

"You know I loved his mother at one time, but she was conniving." Poseidon continued. "What I believed was love was merely her infatuation. She wanted my position, to be wife to me, usurp my power. The Dark Demon who lives in the Marianas Trench came along and made her a better offer and she left me." He swung his arm wide. "And off she went, leaving the boy behind," Poseidon boomed. The vibration sent seashell lights hanging from the ceiling crashing into one another. He shuffled over and sat down on his throne.

"I'll be the first to admit, I wasn't the best guardian for the boy." He rapped on the arm of his chair with his knuckles.

Startled, Ella stepped back. The fact Poseidon had shared so much private information, gave her a tingling in the pit of her stomach, similar to eating a spoiled bowl of chili.

"You, sea witch, are relieved of any obligation to me. I'd be honored if you'll continue in your role of guardian for the coast, but the responsibility is no longer yours." He stared at the floor, dejected.

Ella stepped forward and cautiously placed a hand on Poseidon's arm. "I accept guardianship of the coast. If it pleases Your Highness, would you agree to a tour of my underwater museum before it opens to the public?"

He lifted his head and looked directly into her eyes. His shimmered with tremendous power, and yet he was quiet when he spoke. "Yes, I'll tour your museum, before we leave for Atlantis."

"Thank you, Your Highness." Ella bowed. The joy bubbling up inside her made her want to skip from the throne room. She couldn't wait to tell James and Noah the good news!

Hettie and Evan's wedding was held on Saturday three weeks after their misadventure with Kenn.

A full moon shone down on Noah as he walked from the dock to Ella's house. He would drive her and Mischell to the nuptials. Hettie and Evan had picked the sacred circle by the hemlock tree for their wedding. Tonight would be a full moon and that should bring prosperity and happiness to their union.

Noah inserted the key into the ignition of her old truck and it chugged to life. In a matter of minutes he turned off the main road onto the forest road. Mischell giggled as they bumped along a meandering dirt road leading deep into the forest. The truck rattled and complained as they bumped over uneven ground.

"I've never, ever been to a wedding! Noah, turn on the inside light," Mischell ordered, checking her hair and makeup in her little clam-shaped mirror Ella had bought for her. "This is totally the best day ever. Ella, do you think my lip gloss is dark enough?"

"Yes, you look perfect," she said, stifling a smile behind her hand. "You are fortunate your guardians let you attend the wedding. We can't stay for the reception—we have to get you back in time for your transformation."

"I know, I know," said the disgruntled mermaid. "I'll be glad when I've changed to my final form and can stay on land for longer periods of time, and did Hettie tell you? She said I could have a job at the Crystal Witch when I'm old enough."

"Yes, she did. So you're thinking of living in Waxing part of the time?" Ella held on to the hand grip when the truck hit an especially deep pothole.

"Yeah, won't it be great? Maybe I could stay at your house, Ella?"

"We'll see." Ella smiled. She had grown quite fond of Mischell. The mermaid had shown bravery in the underwater cavern, and had helped Noah subdue Kenn. Ella had been pleased how Mischell had stayed behind refusing to leave Noah till help arrived.

When Hettie announced her wedding date, Ella had petitioned Mischell's guardians for permission to take her for a day of shopping, hair styling and to attend the wedding. Since Mischell had turned fourteen she could stay on land for twelve hours. They'd had great fun together. She was looking forward to the time Mischell could come and stay with her on a semi-permanent basis.

The High Priestess Darla performed the wedding ceremony. Oscar walked Hettie down the aisle. Tears of joy flowed down the cheeks of every member of their coven. Hettie, their sister witch, was the first to find her true love and marry. Afterward, Noah and Ella said their goodbyes and took a tired little mermaid back to Turtle Point.

Noah carried Mischell down the trail to a secluded beach, not because she had changed, but because she was exhausted.

Ella slipped her new red high heels off, and followed Noah, her toes squished in sand with each step. Silver moon light paved the path with light and they had no trouble hiking to the sandy shore.

"I hate leaving," Mischell said, her lip quivering.

"Sweetheart, your guardian promised if you don't run away any more, and mind your lessons, she'll allow you to spend a day with me once a month." Ella hugged her close. "Now here," she handed her the red high heels. "These are for James. And this," she said, pulling a purple embroidered bag out of her purse, "is for you."

"What…for me?"

"Open the bag," Noah said. "I helped pick them out."

Mischell opened the bag, dumping all the contents on a flat rock. Necklaces, bracelets, and rings gleamed and glittered in the moonlight. She slid on a couple rings and bracelets, holding her hand out to admire the bling. "Oh, my, I've never had such beautiful gifts." She stood up, hugged Ella and shyly hugged Noah. "Thank you! What a grand present, best ever." She gathered the remainder of the jewels off the rock and put them back into the bag. Mischell grabbed the shoes and walked to the water's edge. "Bye! I'll never forget today, not ever." She glided into the next wave and changed instantly. She slapped her tail and disappeared into the ocean.

Noah put his arm around Ella, and warmth radiated through her body. "I guess it's time to go." She turned into his embrace, filled to capacity with love for him. He had risked his life to save hers; a human saving a witch.

He had a wide grin on his face. "Not yet." He touched the end of her nose with a fingertip.

"I'm exhausted, from taking Mischell around town today, and the wedding. Let's go home," she pleaded.

"Sit on the rock, Ella; give the boy a chance." James' boomed.

She sat down stiffly, not knowing what to expect. Noah kneeled on the sand in front of her. "Ella, you have turned my world upside down. You've drawn me into a world of Magick and myth, a world I never knew existed. Talking octopus, mermaids and my own sea witch—I love you madly, deeply, I don't ever want to let you go." He leaned in and kissed her. "I know you've said we've bonded, but I want more. I'm asking you to be my wife." His finger under her chin, he tilted her head up. "Ella, my beautiful, smart sea witch, will you marry me?"

Her heart skipped a beat then settled down. She put her hand over her mouth, her eyes filled with tears, threatening to spill over; her vow to not become involved shattered all the way.

"Now is where you are supposed to say 'yes'," he prompted, seeming to enjoy her lack of composure.

"Yes, yes, I'll marry you." She threw her arms around him, catching him off guard and they tumbled to the beach laughing.

Let me be the first to congratulate you two. Tell Noah to hold out his hand; I found what he requested. James chuckled. *You look like two burrowing clams flopping around on the sand.*

Ella relayed his message. Noah laughed and held out his hand. A tentacle emerged from the ocean and plopped a huge diamond ring surrounded by sapphires into his hand.

Tell the boy this ring is from a pirate ship, sunk hundreds of years ago. The ring is one of a kind, like your love. James' choked up. *Goodnight now, and thanks for the lovely shoes.*

Ella transmitted the interpretation to Noah. He slipped the beautiful ring on her finger, a perfect fit. "One of a kind," he murmured. "Just like our love. I like it."

The heartwarming tenderness of his gaze made her spirits soar. He pulled her into his embrace. A Magick glow appeared around them, swirling, lifting them up from the sandy beach. She laughed as stardust sparked around them as if they were in a sparkly snow globe, and Magick carried them back to her truck.

Home, she thought, she was complete. She had the future to look forward to with her man, her lover, her soulmate. What more could she desire?

Bonus Story

The short story "The Crystal Witch", published originally in the anthology "Love & Magick", follows this novella.

Ella first appears in this story, and her story evolved into "The Witch with the Trident Tattoo".

If you want to read the story that started it all I've attached it here as a bonus.

Learn more about me and my books at:

https://dianamccollum.weebly.com/

Anthologies:

"Love & Magick" with Judith Ashley & Sarah Raplee

"Gifts from the Heart" with the Windtree Press authors.

The Crystal Witch

by Diana McCollum

Dedication

For Loyd and my children for all their love, encouragement and support.

Acknowledgements

To my critique partners Sarah McDermed and Louise Pelzl thank you for your generous and honest critiques.

And a huge shout-out to my Bend lunch bunch, writers who didn't mind answering all my questions: Marie Harte, Karen Duvall, Paty Jager, Mary Pax.

Chapter One

October 15, 2012

The right mixture of violet and blue evening sky laced with bolts of scarlet bouncing off the clouds always brought to mind the evening of her death, or what would have been Hettie's death had she not escaped.

Even after ten years in the small coastal town of Waxing, Massachusetts, a death-sky inspired panic deep in her chest. She took several calming breaths, repeating her time-worn mantra.

"'Tis a frivolous fear, for naught dangerous be near. Bless this house, bless this store, bless me ever more." Hettie intoned the mantra three times.

She put a match to bundled sage twigs and walked the boundary of her small gift shop, the Crystal Witch. Climbing the stairs to her apartment, at the door she murmured an opening charm and crossed the threshold then proceeded to walk the length of every wall, in every room. The blessed smoke from the stems both cleansed and protected the space. She stopped by the front window. Pulling the lace curtain aside, she looked out at the sky, almost dark now. The shadow of a figure merged with the dark of the woods across the street. Did she see a lonely soul out for an evening walk, or something more sinister? Her stomach clenched; it could be time to pay her debt.

Samhain was approaching. The time of year when the veil between worlds was easily accessible, when good or evil could pass through with barely a ripple in the curtain. Hettie was uneasy this time of year, and with good reason; if Declan came for her, it would be during this preternatural time.

He'd have to find her first. He didn't know where Shaman Adahy had sent her. If Declan knew where she was, he would have come for her. This she knew without a doubt. One didn't make a deal with the devil unless one was willing to pay the price.

After taking the small ceramic pots of spearmint and peppermint off the window sill and placing them on the counter, Hettie closed the curtain. Gathering a wooden spoon, small pan and mesh strainer she set about brewing a calming tea. The ritual of making tea at the end of a busy day comforted her. She gently removed leaves from the plants, washed them, and put the sprigs in the pot sitting on the stove. In the pantry she took a jar of dried chamomile off the shelf. A teaspoon of chamomile went in the pan.

She took the wooden spoon, pressing the leaves against the side of the pot, bruising the herbs. She closed her eyes and breathed in the released aroma. She added two cups of water and turned the stove on.

Hettie stirred until the pot bubbled briskly, and then removed the wooden spoon. Holding her hands over the steam she spoke.

With plants of earth I make this tea,
Charged with magick to its task;
May the Goddess in me,
Help me relax,
So mote it be.

Hettie gently settled the lid on the pot, turned the fire down for the required half hour of steeping.

She changed into her favorite silk pajamas, and pulled on her fleece bathrobe to fend off the evening chill. Taking a mug out of the cupboard she poured the steaming tea into the cup. She sat in the maple rocking chair, her favorite one, the rocker which reminded her of Mama's. She sipped the hot brew and closed her eyes.

Chapter Two

October 30, 1692
Waxing, MA

The day in the village of Waxing began as a quiet fall morning, with a break in the rain which had plummeted from the sky for the past several days. Henrietta took the pail off the hook by the hearth and left to fetch the morning water. She was sixteen years now and considered a woman. Papa had died in a hunting accident last year and Gram shortly after. Now there was just her and Mama. The depression that had plagued Mama since Papa's death was consuming her, and Henrietta helplessly watched Mama shrink a little more each day.

Henrietta had prayed to the goddess asking for help in the matter of her mother's illness. The Goddess had come to Henrietta in a dream last night, and told her to go into the woods on the full moon, to the sacred circle, and Mama would be cured. Tonight was a full moon and Henrietta was determined to follow the instructions from her vision.

She worked the squeaky crank on the well, pulling up a fresh bucket of water, and lifting it over the edge and then dumped the water into her own pail.

"Ho, Henrietta, I'll carry your bucket," said Waya. He picked up her pail, his arm muscles bulging under the weight. "Have you time for a lesson?"

Waya, the Cherokee shaman's son, was a few years older than her. She had been instructing Waya in his letters for several months now. In return, he brought venison, birds and grains for her and Mama. If not for Waya, they might have starved. He was a great hunter just like his namesake, the wolf.

"Of course, I have time for you. Mama needs her morning meal first. Come along and you can join us." His nearness sent a shiver up her spine. They had grown close over the past few months and the bond went both ways. She felt good in his company, safe; yes, she felt safe. He'd kissed her a few times. She would welcome more. She glanced sideways at him.

They were careful with their friendship, since personal association with anyone from the tribe was frowned upon by the community elders.

Waya had kissed her yesterday. Not the quick kiss, friendly thank you type of kiss, but a passionate kiss. She had daydreamed of being crushed in his embrace; their clandestine relationship was the most thrilling thing to ever happen to her. Thinking about the kiss sent butterflies fluttering in her stomach.

Yesterday she would have made flummery save for the lack of sea moss and milk, two key ingredients. Then she could have served the pudding to Waya this morning.

They reached the picket fence and Waya set the pail of water down.

"Do you have chores, Henrietta? I can help today." He scrunched up his forehead, searching for the right words. "I have no teachings today from Adahy. I am free as the —," he said turning his hand in the air, fluttering his fingers, "bird." He smiled and his eyes twinkled; he looked quite pleased for finding the proper words.

"Henrietta!" Declan Blackthorn called out, his tone disapproving.

"Yes?" She turned to see the preacher's son barreling down on them.

"What are you doing with this heathen?" Declan looked Waya up and down. "He's barely dressed! Cover yourself, man. Henrietta is a decent God fearing woman and you dare to seek out her company?" Hands on hips and long black coat flapping around his legs, he was an imposing sight at six foot and five inches. He was older than Henrietta by five years.

"I'm helping him with his handwriting and reading proficiencies. Declan, he is good to Mama and me. He brings us venison and other food. Otherwise we would have starved after father perished!" Such a fury boiled inside her, it churned in her stomach and rose up to her heart, increasing the rhythm of the beat till she thought her heart could surely be heard by both men. She must keep her fury restrained; she summoned her will power and tried again. "Declan, sir, step away from us, begone."

"Get out of here, heathen, and don't come back." Declan flung his arm wide and pointed toward the woods.

Waya seemed to grow taller in front of her eyes. He was majestic with his long black braids, muscular chest and snapping black eyes.

"Ho, Henrietta, I wish to cause you no trouble. The tree we talked of…." Waya touched the carved bone moon hanging on a beaded cord around his neck. He tipped his head slightly in acknowledgment, turned and walked toward the woods.

I'll be there tonight, at the full moon, Waya's voice whispered in her head.

Henrietta, stunned to have heard Waya's silent words, could only stare at his retreating back. She turned back to Declan so fast her long skirts flared out. "What is wrong with you? He is human like us, and he is very nice. You have no reason to treat him so."

"He is the shaman's son. There is devil magick there and you'd best watch what magick you want to be associated with." Declan walked around her looking her up and down, measuring her like one of his prize horses. His boot landed in a puddle and sprayed the edge of her dress with muddied water.

"And what would you know of magick, Declan? Aren't you the preacher's son? Isn't magick the devil's tool?" Her hands balled up, her arms shook in a desperate attempt to control the building rage.

His green eyes flashing, he leaned in close to her till their noses almost touched, so close in fact she counted three small hairs growing out of the mole on his left cheek.

"I know of magick. I know of magick in your family, Henrietta. Watch your back," he spat out. He turned and took his leave.

The fury rolled out of her extended hands, scooping up the muddy puddle and slamming it against Declan's back with the intensity of an Atlantic Ocean wave, sending him hurling to the ground.

"What... who... did that?" Sputtered Declan. He wiped his muddied hands on his wet coat.

Henrietta grabbed the pail of well water, passed through the gate, and hurried through the door. She set the pail on the floor and leaned against the wooden door.

This was the year when her magickal abilities would reach full force. Gram had told her what to expect. Mama didn't know. The powers were passed down to the firstborn girl on her father's side of the family. The magick had been showing up in bits and pieces. Was the fury now coursing through her part of the magick? And how could she hear what Waya whispered in her head?

One thing was clear; Henrietta would be at the hemlock tree tonight, right after she visited the sacred circle.

Mama was standing in the middle of the room, a vacant expression on her face. Henrietta hastened over and took hold of her arm. "Come, Mama, sit in the rocker. I'll fix you some porridge."

# # #

The afternoon was spent practicing spells. She could conjure fire, heal a cut and mend a slash with nothing but an incantation and her will. Gram had given her the family Tome of Magick. Gram said to memorize as many spells, curses and hexes as possible. Once she knew how they worked, Henrietta could create her own as needed.

She sat now in her mother's rocker thumbing through the tome. This morning's demonstration of her awakening power gave her hope she could work a spell to relieve her mother's great grief.

She sighed. Nothing. There was nothing she could do, no quick magick spell that would fix her mama.

She tried to send out several thoughts to Waya. No response. Their connection would be an area she needed to work on.

Chapter Three

Henrietta reached the sacred circle at the apex of the full moon. She set her candles on the four points of the directions of the wind, east, west, north and south. She slipped out of her clothes and let the moonlight bathe her. She chanted the welcoming song to the Goddess. Dancing and swaying in the moonlight, bringing forth power from the circle, she sang an incantation, and then put into the world her request for Mama's recovery. She ended her invocation, bared to the moon, arms outstretched, when she saw Waya standing beneath the hemlock at the edge of the circle. She was not embarrassed; it was as it should be, and she welcomed him into the circle.

He discarded the deer hide breech clout and leggings. The moon totem on a leather thong around his neck, the only thing he wore as he stepped into the sacred circle. He brushed her long hair from her breasts and laid it over her shoulders to hang down her back.

His hands moved magickly over her breasts; she was shocked by her own eager response to his touch. The touch of his lips on hers sent a shockwave of passion through her body that pooled in her woman parts. He eased her down to the grass. "Henrietta, I have desired you since I first saw you. Is this joining what you wish too?"

Heat of the craving they shared warmed her. She nodded, too delirious with passion to speak. She surrendered herself to his seduction and together they burned with desire.

Later they lay naked and still, moist from their lovemaking, too tired to move. She wanted to stay here forever with her lover.

"Little one, I've had a vision. You will be leaving." He raised her hand to his lips.

"No. I'm not going anywhere."

"Evil is coming." He stood and gave her a hand up. "You must leave this place. No matter — I will find you. Wherever you are, I will find you. Don't fear. Be brave, little one. You have the magick in you and this is what will keep you safe." His eyes were hooded like those of a hawk. "We have mated. I am yours, you are mine."

"I want to be with you forever, Waya. Surely Mama and I could dwell with you. I could be with you, and we could live with the tribe?" Her eyes threatened to spill tears down her cheeks.

"No. Evil has already visited your home this night. Get your things and meet me by the Hemlock tree. We will find a way to protect you." He settled her dress over her shoulders. "My totem." He took off the bone moon necklace and placed the cord around her neck. "Wear this always, and if we are parted, I will find you." His kiss sent new waves of ecstasy through her.

Chapter Four

She ran through the woods toward home. The autumn air was cool on skin still hot from loving Waya.

The loud, frightening voices of zealous townsmen halted her on the edge of the woods. A parade of torches marched from her house toward the town square. What was going on?

Henrietta ran after them, her hair flying behind her. She grabbed the arm of her neighbor, Amy Scotts. "Why were they at my home? Where is everyone going?"

"Henrietta, you were gone. The men came and took your mama to jail. She was called a hag and charged with witchcraft." Henrietta's stomach churned with fright at the panic in Amy's voice.

The fools didn't understand the great grief that had struck Mama and said instead her soul had been claimed by the devil and she was his servant now.

"Amy, you know mama is struck by melancholy right now. You *know*, Amy!"

"Let go of me, lest I scream for assistance." Amy wrenched her arm away. "We know the mind is the feeblest when downheartedness strikes. I'm sorry your mama succumbed to the devil. Declan said today she threw muddied water with such force it knocked him down."

"Declan lies!" Tears burned a trail down Henrietta's cheeks.

"Watch yourself! To call the preacher's son a liar is blasphemous." Amy spun away and hurried after the townspeople.

Henrietta stood in the middle of the street. Waya had been right. Evil had visited her home tonight. There had to be a way to save her mother. The elders spurred by Declan had accused many and hung some declared to be witches. Her heart beat a rapid tattoo. She couldn't let this happen to her mama.

Inside her house, she grabbed the Tome of Magick and wrapped it in her shawl. She crept out of the house. The shouting of the angry villagers faded away, and only then did Hettie venture past her gate. She snuck past the dwellings of the townspeople, quiet now, all snug in their homes. She stayed out of the moonlight instead seeking out the shadows till she reached the window of the jail cell where Mama was being held.

"*Psst. Psst.* Mama!" Henrietta grasped the metal bar and pulled herself up to peer inside.

"Henrietta, dear child, I don't understand, why have they taken me? Where am I?" Mama asked, her face a mixture of uncertainty and awareness.

"Mama, you're better. My prayers have been answered." Henrietta choked out. To have her mother healthy only to be hung at the gallows on the morrow was more than she could bear. The witch trials were short and punishment by hanging swiftly executed. She had to do something to save her mama.

"Better? Was I ill?" She grasped the metal bars wrapping her hands over Henrietta's

"Papa died and you've been suffering terrible ever since," Henrietta said.

"But why have they put me in jail?" The moonlight shone through the window on Mama's face, her brow creased with worry.

"They are accusing you of being a witch, having sold your soul to the devil. Mama, I have to get you out of there." She jerked on the metal bars in frustration.

Henrietta felt his presence before his arm came around her waist, pulling her up against him. His hand over her mouth, Declan said in a rasping voice, "I can save your mother. But in return you have to give me something I want. Something I need."

She nodded yes, anything, she'd do anything to save her mother from the hangman's noose.

"If I remove my hand from your mouth, do you promise not to yell?" His whispered words were hot in her ear.

She nodded yes. Tears welled in her eyes, spilling over. He removed his hand and readjusted his arm around her waist, pulling her even tighter against him. With his free hand, he brushed her hair away from her neckline and ran his tongue up and down her neck. "What I want from you" — he nipped at her neck with his teeth — "is your magick power."

Henrietta drew deep inside herself for calm; to show fear in the face of evil would give him more power. This was not the Declan she knew. Since Gram had introduced her to the world of magick, she had been aware there were things in this world she knew nothing of — things of both joy and evil. Gram had said *evil walks among us.*

"I have no magick power." She closed her eyes and breathed deep. She must remain calm to help Mama.

"Ah-h, but you do. The first daughter of each generation of your father's family has power, and that my dear, would be you." Another nip of his teeth sent pain searing through her skin.

"Even if I had such power, magick, I'd not know how to give it to you." Her heart beat so loud and fast she was sure he could hear it, but she kept her voice steady.

"Do you want to save your mother from hanging in the gallows tomorrow?" He shook her.

"Yes." His grip sent shock waves through her.

"Do you want your mother to live?"

"Yes!"

He turned her around and holding her shoulders, lifted her with strength not of this world until her feet swung like a rag doll. His eyes blazed like green glass, the only color in the gray, moonlit landscape. "Henrietta Anne Wynn, do you pledge to come to me of your own free will when your mother is safe from further persecution?"

"Yes!" With this final '*yes*' she had made her deal with Declan. The power of three would be next to impossible to break.

Declan let loose of her and she dropped to the ground in a heap. The structure holding the cell dissolved in a cloud of dust and smoke. Mama sat on the ground beside her, and wrapped Henrietta in a comforting embrace.

Declan stood with one arm outstretched towards the destroyed building. He chanted in a tongue unfamiliar to Henrietta.

Mama gasped as the rubble rose up into the air and rebuilt the jail.

"I have wiped the memories of the events of this night from the fair citizen's minds." Declan turned on his heel and disappeared in a cloud of fog.

"Mama?" The tears spilled over and she looked into Mama's eyes, no longer vacant but full of concern.

"It's all right. He's gone. Let's go home." She smoothed Henrietta's hair.

How could Declan destroy the building that held Mama? What had he said to her? *Do you pledge to come to me of your own free will?* She needed to get Mama home and go meet Waya. His father, Adahy, was the Shaman. He would know what to do. She fingered the moon totem. She would need all the help she could get to break the curse of giving herself to Declan.

Chapter Five

Sun broke over the treetops, painting the trees with a profusion of autumn colors. Henrietta pulled her cloak tighter against the chill that sent goose bumps up her arms. Pine needles and fallen autumn leaves crushed underfoot sent a pungent smell into the air. The Hemlock tree was not far from the path. She sat on an old stump near the meeting site. The forest was quiet now, and she watched the morning unfold.

Birds began their morning chirping and flying to and fro. Fall had come late this year and many trees had not yet lost their vibrant leaves. The forest was waking up. Her eyes closed, she concentrated on all the life currents around her. A rustle in the fallen leaves, the babbling brook, and the hum of insects not yet taken by the frost; she had all the elements she would need. Magick was part will, part tokens and conjuring. A leaf here, a twig there, her crystal wand and the right spell. All different incantations took the assistance of different bits and pieces.

Tonight was Samhain. According to Gran's book, this was the strongest night for magick. This was a night the veil was thin between the mortal and magickal realms. Perfect. Tonight she'd somehow escape Declan and her pledge.

She heard a footstep on the path and opened her eyes.

"Waya!" She ran to him and into his waiting embrace. "Something terrible has happened. The townspeople called Mama a witch and were going to hang her. Declan has an evil power in him and made me promise to come to him, and in exchange he would save Mama."

"What did you answer, little one?" He gently rubbed her back.

"I'm sorry, Waya, I had to answer *yes*. I had to save Mama."

A muscle quivered in his jaw. "Declan is a powerful dark witch who spouts dark magick. He is trying to become a force to be reckoned with. The witches who were accused by Declan and the elders, and hung, he inherited their life forces. He is stronger for it."

"He's the preacher's son! How can this be?"

"Declan is no longer the preacher's son. When I looked into his eyes yesterday, it was not Declan who stared back, but pure evil. Another entity has taken over his soul." Waya set her away from him. "We must devise a way to save you until you are strong enough, powerful enough, and clever enough to not just oppose him, but win the battle with him."

"He said he wants me to come to him of my own free will. Mama is safe. That cannot be changed, can it?" Her heart skipped a beat, and a chill raced up her spine at the thought of Mama sinking back into her depression. Her recovery was due to the Goddess and could not be undone by Declan.

Shaman Adahy walked towards them from the woods. "Henrietta, you know the power of three. Declan asked you three times and you answered three times. The magick he performed saving your mother is sealed for eternity. Your pact with the witch Declan is not sealed. To give him control of your magick you must do so willingly. There are consequences if you don't follow through. But the outcome can be altered."

The old Shaman leaned heavily on his medicine staff. Adahy waved one hand around the expanse of the clearing. "There is powerful magick here. I was favored by your Grandmother. We had a bond of harmony and worked together on many enchantments. She performed much of her magick in this space, as did I. Because of her and what came before this time, we will make great magick on this hallowed ground." He lifted his staff overhead. The feathers bound by leather thongs danced in the light fall breeze. He turned in a full circle, chanting in his native tongue.

Henrietta was mesmerized by the Shaman's dance. Waya laid a hand on her shoulder and they both watched. "Father is asking the great spirit to show us humble beings a way to fight this evil."

Adahy thumped his medicine staff against the forest floor three times. He stood head bowed for a moment, then lifted his head.

His sage face fairly creased with wisdom. "It has been shown to me, Henrietta, you are a powerful witch, like your Grandmother. Waya too, a mighty warrior and seeker of justice, has great magick to fight this evil. The struggle comes tonight and will take all three of us if you are to survive." He walked toward the cover of the woods.

"What will we do?" She was sure the men could hear the rapid beat of her heart.

Adahy stopped and looked over his shoulder. "Before the day is done, while the sun makes the journey into night, we will meet here at your sacred circle. There all will be decided. Go now, prepare for the meeting. Declan will have no choice but to be there, this my vision has shown." He turned and disappeared into the thick woods.

"Henrietta." Waya cupped her chin. His expression stilled as he leaned in and kissed her. "Be brave, little one. I have much to do before we meet tonight. Stay in your house till then. Declan can only come in if you ask him to."

"I will. And, Waya?"

"Yes?"

"Thank you for telling Adahy and asking for his help."

"I didn't. He knew from his visions. Come, I'll walk you back."

Chapter Six

Tonight's ritual would take all the power Henrietta could summon. She practiced protection spells, chants and charms while Mama, with the help of a relaxing tea, slept the day away. In the middle of learning how to summon the power dwelling deep inside of her, there was a rap on the door.

She drew in a calming breath, and spoke through the door, "Who's there?"

"Henrietta, it's me, Declan, open up." His voice was young again, not the harsh rasp of last night.

"No, Mama is ill. She's sleeping." She crossed her fingers against the lie, that it might not wreak mayhem with her magick. "Declan, do you remember last night? What happened between us?"

"I didn't see you last night I was in bed before dark. Come out, walk with me," he pleaded. "Tell me Waya is not in there. You shouldn't be seen in his company."

"No, Waya is not here, and no, I'll not walk with you. Go away." Convinced the evil spirit lingered inside him, she wasn't going to take any chances.

She waited by the door until his footsteps on the graveled path faded. The candle on the table flamed to life with a flick of her hand. Another hour and she'd leave for the sacred circle. She had studied the book, memorized what she could, and tried spells she could do inside. She would pen a letter to Mama telling her she was going away for a while. With Mama's health restored by the Goddess, Declan having wiped the witchcraft charge out of the villager's minds, Hettie knew her Mother would be fine.

Picking up a quill, Henrietta penned a missive telling her Mama she needed to go away for her own safety, and not to worry.

She charmed a totem with a protection spell, with instructions her mama should wear it always. They had discussed Declan, witches and all that had transpired the night before.

She moved the candle to the hearth and spread her shawl on the trestle table. Gathering the Tome of Magick, candles, crystal wand, and sacred rocks, she placed them on her shawl and bound the bundle up tight. Dressed in her black wool dress, her unruly hair in a tight bun with various tendrils escaping even now, she slipped her cape over her shoulders, pulled the hood up, picked up her bundle and tiptoed out the door.

# # #

The evening sky was fantastically full of color. Just the right mixture of violet and blue laced with bolts of scarlet bouncing off the clouds. The sky was crimson only with deeper more passionate colors. She stopped at the edge of the woods to admire the sunset and breathe in the scent of the pines. She shifted her bundle on her shoulder and entered the woods. She found it dark and hard to see in the forest. It didn't matter, she knew where to go. She'd been there a hundred times since Gram had given her the spell book. She missed Gram; her passing came soon after Papa's and had left an empty space in her heart.

Waya and Adahy were at the circle and had built a fire.

"We will guard the circle and you." Waya took her cape from her, folding and placing it in the circle.

"I must prepare the sacred space without you. The circle must be consecrated for the goddess to attend." She felt blessed they had come.

"We know this. Rest assured we will protect you. I have spread the essential herbs around the edge of the ring. The fire will ward off animals and all spirits that have an aversion to flame."

Adahy began his chant and dance around the circle for protection. Waya carried her bundle to the circle. His ebony eyes sparkled with the reflection of the firelight. "Father has worked a ritual that will see you safe in another place until Declan can be dealt with. I'll find you." He lifted the totem hanging around her neck. "Rub this when you need extra power." He pressed the bone moon against her chest and stepped back away out of the circle.

The fire crackled and popped, sending a spray of sparks skyward.

Waya's bronze skin glistened in the firelight, giving the impression he was made of gold. A black tattoo of a wolf decorated his arm and the eyes seemed alive in the light from the blaze. He was magnificent and he was hers. She believed with all her heart they would be together one day.

"What are you doing?" roared Declan, as he lumbered from the woods. His long black coat flapped with each stride. "Come out of the circle, Henrietta. You owe me!" He prowled around the circle ranting on until he came face to face with Waya.

Henrietta began chanting, with her arms lifted towards the stars. She turned with her eyes closed visualized a safe place, a place not unlike Waxing, where she lived now. A place without Declan, a place where she could live and be safe.

She opened her eyes to see Waya push Declan to the ground and advance on him. Declan jumped up, hand out-stretched and sent a bolt of light energy knocking Waya down. In a matter of seconds Declan spun around stalking the shaman.

Adahy's fevered singing reached a high pitch, almost a screech.

Waya yelled, "No! Father!"

She turned in the circle, still chanting, reaching the end of her spell. Adahy pointed his staff at her and a bolt of energy swept over her, knocking her down. The last thing she saw before the engulfing darkness was Adahy crumbling to the ground with Declan's knife sticking out of his chest.

Chapter Seven

October 16, 2012
Waxing, MA

Hettie woke with a start. She glanced at the clock on the wall. It was well past midnight, two in the morning to be exact. A whiff of smoke and pine assaulted her nose. She checked her sage wand where it lay spent on the iron, leaf-shaped plate. Could the smells be remnants of her dream?

Waya — what had become of him? Did Adahy die from the blade Declan stuck in him? She would give anything to know, but the chances of her ever knowing were slim to none. She fingered the moon talisman; she always wore.

Setting her cup in the sink, she looked out the window at the sliver of moon. There would be a hunter's moon by Samhain. She wanted to try a new spell when magick was the strongest, a seeing spell. Instead of the future, she wanted to see into the past.

She stood and stretched and entered the bedroom. A flick of her hand and the drapes closed. The Tiffany lamp flickered on and soft melodious music filled the air. This was her sanctuary. She had arranged her altar against the wall in front of a small octagonal window facing the arc of the moon; the light shining in now made her crystal wand glow. It had never been a straight wand, always a bit bent on the end, and the shaft had four smooth sides instead of being round. The wand had traveled from England on a schooner with Gram to the new world, to Waxing.

The rod of crystal had been Gram's and Gram's mother's before her, and passed down through the ages till Gram had placed the wand in Hettie's hands along with the Tome of Magick.

Moonlight empowered the wand, and it grew stronger each passing cycle. She rarely used her wand. Once in a while she would visit the sacred circle in the woods, always alone, the same one she had used all those centuries ago. The ancient hemlock tree was still alive; it appeared healthy and strong, and she was sure great magick dwelled deep inside. Waya and Adahy had used the tree in many of their supernatural invocations. She hadn't witnessed this, but Waya had told her many stories of the great tree and how it was a significant part of their rituals. Even Adahy and Gram had shared their rituals and magick beneath the great branches.

The forest was alive, and Hettie knew where every berry bush, mushroom and toad lived. They were her woods. Thanks to the Historic Landscape Preservation Program the woods were safe from loggers and the encroachment of towns. Waxing, being a small community, and was focused on the fishing industry. Not many people wandered the forest paths. The woods were her sanctuary. That's where she would go on Samhain.

She snuggled down in her bed, appreciating the pillow top mattress. She pulled the dark blue comforter up. Picking up *Techniques for Dating Mr. Right*, she opened it to the bookmark. Relationships had eluded her in this new world. She dated a few different guys over the years, but none of the relationships had clicked. Her fault, she guessed.

Hettie had led an isolated life since she arrived here. The less anyone knew about her the better. She wasn't a good liar, so she kept her life simple and safe. She longed for love, comfort and connection. Who wouldn't? After ten years in the new world, who was she kidding? Unless he fell in her lap, she'd probably never meet Mr. Right.

Determined to make a change in her love life, she began reading.

"Try something new. Take up jogging, it's healthy and you never know who you will run into. Are you a TV buff? Go out to a movie instead, and stop at the local coffee shop for a late night latte.

Learn a new skill. Golf, bowling, archery or ballroom dancing are great ways to meet singles." She slammed the book shut.

Kitty chose that moment to jump up on the bed. The big orange cat purred and kneaded the blankets. Kitty was another lost soul Aunt Bea had taken in not long before she'd found Hettie wandering, lost and confused, in the woods nearby. She'd opened her heart and home to Hettie when no family could be found. Aunt Bea had called Hettie's condition *amnesia,* and Hettie had been relieved when Aunt had stopped asking her questions about her past.

Hettie could picture Aunt Bea with her silver hair, shaking her finger and saying, "I have no family. Now I have you. We are family, us and Kitty." Then she'd embrace Hettie in a warm loveable hug.

Aunt Bea had left the shop, apartment and a small inheritance to her. Hettie was eternally grateful for Aunt Bea's generosity, and missed her every day.

"Kitty, you're my good boy." Petting him was soothing. "You miss her too, don't you?" The tension eased out of her shoulders. Her eyes began to droop and she felt sleep coming on.

Chapter Eight

Halloween would be here soon. Hettie worked on decorating her shop. She enjoyed Halloween and the costumed children, the cute little witches, vampires and superheroes; it didn't matter to her, she loved them all. This year she had placed an order for an extra special treat for the children, miniature crystal witches holding a crystal wand and a broom. She would bless each one to protect the children on Samhain. This would be a happy day and a dangerous one with the curtain between worlds thin.

She longed for a child of her own. Deep in her heart, she knew she'd never have a family. Unless she put herself out in the, what was it called in the book? The dating game.

She plugged in the purple twinkle lights that hung around the storefront window and stepped back to admire her work. Yes, she liked the lights. Kitty, curled up sleeping in his cat bed in the store window, added to the overall Halloween theme. The public would expect a black cat. Orange would have to do. Besides, he complimented the Jack-O-Lantern in the window.

She waved her hand and set light to the spice candles sitting on the counter and display cases. All her candles were made by Ella, her friend, and occasional employee.

Hettie would have to order more candles from Ella as sales had picked. The wonderful smelling and long lasting harvest candles were flying off the shelf. She wrote on her list of things to do *call Ella*. Maybe Ella would have the candles ready by Saturday when the coven was scheduled to meet.

The delivery door buzzer rang. Hettie opened the door to a tall man, easy smile, dark hair, and warm cinnamon skin. Not old Mr. Tuttle, her usual delivery man.

"Where's Mr. Tuttle?"

"He's been assigned a desk job. Hurt his back last week. I have a couple of boxes you'll need to sign for." He handed her the electronic signature board.

She signed her name as he carried the boxes in one by one and stacked them in her small storeroom.

The last box was not squarely on top. Kitty chose that moment to meander over and leap on the top box, causing it to tip over, and crash to the floor. Emitting a loud '*meow*' he scampered off.

"Sounds like something broke. Let me open it up and we'll do a damage assessment." He pulled out a box knife.

"No! Everything is fine." Hettie leaned over and mumbled an incantation, placing her hands on the center of the damaged box, repairing the broken goods. There wasn't time to return the broken merchandize and have new ones sent by Samhain.

"Look, lady, this is my job. I heard something break. We need to assess the damage."

"Okay." She glanced at his name tag. "Mr. Wolf."

"Evan."

"Evan, then," she liked the sound of his name.

He opened the box and a look of wonder crossed his face. His brows puckered together. "Looks like all the little… witches are intact. Sure sounded like they all broke. Shattered."

He looked at Hettie, really looked at her. His look seemed to appreciate her as a woman. Her heart missed a beat. His obsidian eyes crinkled at the corners. His mouth was full and his cheekbones high. A ruggedly handsome face, not the face of youth, but a mature looking man, and for a moment she thought this would be how Waya would have aged.

Take a chance, said a little voice in her head. "Would you have time for a cup of coffee or tea while I pack up a few items from the last order I need to return?" The words had flown from her mouth, and now she couldn't take them back.

He took a quick look at his watch. "Sure, coffee would be great. It's about time for a break."

Evan Wolf followed her through the hallway to her office area. She poured coffee into a mug bearing the words *Witches are people too.*

His fingers touched hers and she had the wildest urge to jump back. Maybe this was a mistake, inviting him in. She put a box on the desk, started wrapping bubble wrap around a music box. "I'm Hettie I own this shop, the Crystal Witch." She smiled and secured the package with the mailing tape, then handed it to him.

# # #

Evan held the box. Had she felt that jolt of electricity when he accidentally touched her fingers? She had the most intense blue eyes, set off by wild, long, curly black hair. Nothing tame about this woman.

"Would you be free for lunch or dinner tomorrow?" He was curious how she'd respond after seeing the look of puzzlement on her face when he asked the question.

"I...."

It was too soon; he should never have asked her out. What was wrong with him? He just met the woman. "I'm sorry I put you on the spot. Maybe another time?" What a fool he was.

"No, it's all right. I would like to have dinner with you. Tomorrow night will work for me. Ella Stone looks after the shop on Tuesday evenings." She smiled and the glow warmed him.

"Small world. Ella is a friend of my cousin, Darla Blackfeather. Do you know her?"

"Yes, I do. Darla is wonderful person. She never mentioned you to me. I only say that because she's always trying to fix me up with a date."

He chuckled. "That sounds like Darla. I finished my tour with the Marines a couple weeks ago. Just got back in town, so she hasn't had time to set me up with anyone either."

"What time should I pick you up?" He couldn't stop staring at her mouth, especially when her pink tongue darted out to wet those full lips. He shook his head; what the hell? She oozed sexuality.

"I can leave at six o'clock when Ella gets here." Her high-heeled red boots clicked on the tile floor behind him as she followed him to the door.

"See you then," he looked over his shoulder at a picture of perfection. She was the whole package, curly black hair, tight black dress and killer red boots, and *he* had a date with her.

Chapter Nine

Evan checked his watch, right on time. He parked his car and hit the security lock. Around the corner and two doors down from the Crystal Witch, cinnamon and cloves tickled his nose. The bell over the door sang out when he entered. Purple lights in the window cast a festive luminous light into the shop. The crystal witches he'd delivered yesterday were standing in neat rows by the Jack-O-Lantern in the front window. There must have been a couple of hundred of the three inch glass witches. He couldn't imagine Hettie selling that many in the next couple of weeks.

"May I help you?" Ella finished cleaning her eye glasses and put them on. "Evan Wolf! You're Hettie's date?"

"That would be me, the date. I'm here to take Hettie to dinner." He held out his hand.

She placed her dainty hand in his big one, and then pulled him close for a hug, "You be good to my friend. Don't go breaking her heart you gorgeous man, you." She squeezed his hand before letting go.

"Ella, are you trying to scare my date away?" Hettie said, with a laugh as she emerged from the office at the back of the store.

He couldn't take his eyes off her. She'd been in his dream last night. He had tasted those sweet lips and tangled his hands in her curly ebony hair. And all she wore was the red high heeled boots she wore yesterday, and which she sported now. A tight, mid-calf autumn green dress accentuated her smooth curves, and a black beaded shawl was the icing on the cake. Her hair was pulled back in some kind of twist and secured on her head with an ornamental clip which sparkled when she turned to hand Ella a slip of paper.

"My candle order, I can't keep the harvest ones on the shelf."

"I'm glad to hear that! I'll have a new batch ready by tomorrow. Do you want any special infusions?" Ella took a pen off the counter.

"The same order as before will do. Thanks, see you tomorrow."

That clip would have to come out, he decided. She had a slim, wild, unearthly beauty with her hair trying to escape from the clasp, cobalt eyes and skin like bone china. "You look beautiful." He crooked his arm and she slipped her hand through. Even through the layers of clothes, he felt a jolt of electricity. Was it just him, or did she feel it too? "How does Italian sound?" He guided her across the cross walk.

"Love Italian!" She squeezed his arm, sending another shock through him. "There's a really good restaurant a short walk from here. You game?" He winked at her. She laughed, "I'm game."

Chapter Ten

By Saturday Hettie was on cloud nine. She'd been out of her comfort zone and on a date with Evan every night this past week. He didn't mind waiting for her to close up the shop. They laughed and had such a good time together. Tonight was the coven meeting. She had a date with Evan on Sunday, but she didn't know if she could wait that long. Since she met him, her body seemed to be supercharged. Ella told her she needed to get laid. Maybe that was it. All she knew was the mere thought of Evan sent her heart racing and her nether region tingling, almost inducing a self-inflicted orgasm.

Sunday was a long twenty-four hours away. Her longing for Evan was outside the norm. She knew this, but didn't have a logical explanation for this feeling. She feared she would explode if they didn't make love soon.

Tonight she'd be with the coven, her friends. She still practiced her craft. She had learned to control her power. The local coven of five witches had welcomed her among them. Hettie practiced as a gray witch. *Do no harm* was her creed. However, she would defend herself and those she cared about with whatever means available to her. Luckily, nothing had happened in Waxing to force her to try out the fighting spells she'd learned. She joined the coven and attended the monthly meetings, mostly for the companionship.

She picked up the feather duster and made her way around the shop. She selected one of Mae's handmade soaps off the display table.

Mae, the first coven witch she'd met, made wonderful healing soaps. Hettie held the cheerfully wrapped bar to her nose and breathed in the calming lavender essence. Ella, her good friend and sister witch, created the most amazing aroma therapy candles, and Hettie had a hard time keeping up with the demand.

She ran the duster over the few candles left on the shelf, then continued to the teas nestled in the bookcase display stand. The tea blends made by Ivy, the youngest member of the coven, were medicinal and in high demand as the teas worked exceptionally well. Often Hettie would take special orders for teas to treat different afflictions.

Kitty rubbed up against her legs and "Meowed".

"I know, you're ready for some dinner and comfy time. I'm almost done tidying up."

Kitty gave a final "Meow" and headed upstairs to wait for his mistress.

She gathered the papers on her desk, mostly spell and incantation notes, and put them in her red briefcase.

The door buzzer rang. Dang, she had meant to lock up five minutes ago. A cool breeze swirled around her legs and sent shivers racing up her spine until the small hairs on her neck stood up as if electrified.

The customer turned and headed toward her, his long coat flapping around his legs, his hands stuffed into deep pockets.

"Sorry, I'm closed. I forgot to lock the door."

He looked at her from under the hood of his coat. His face shadowed.

He took a step closer. There was something familiar about his stance.

"You'll have to come back tomorrow. The shop is closed for today." She grabbed the keys out of her pocket and marched toward him.

He threw back his hood. "Hello, Henrietta." His mouth curved up in a deadly grin. His green eyes, sharp as emeralds bore into her.

She had dreaded the day she would hear that voice again. Declan! She tried to move around him, but he grabbed her and threw her up against the wall. Her stomach churned. She had to get away.

"It's your turn to fulfill our little bargain. It wasn't nice to leave as you did. I had to kill that old Indian. He finished his invocation before he died, useless old man."

Declan's nostrils flared and his breath was hot on her face even from the two feet that separated them.

Her heart galloped as she ran for the back of the store; he was there before her. All that stood between them was an oak table full of handmade soaps. She mumbled a quick spell and the soap dissolved into hot liquid. The melted liquid ran down on to Declan's shoes and a hissing noise rose as the molten soap burned holes in his shoes, scorching his feet.

Declan screamed in agony, hopping about, trying to get away from the hexed soap.

Hettie grabbed her briefcase and cell then ran out the back door. In her car, driving away from the shop, she called 9-1-1 to report a break in.

She needed help and fast. She drove to Ella's house. The bungalow was dark; Ella must have left for the coven meeting. Hettie put the car in gear and drove to Darla's house, the High Priestess of the coven. The windows were ablaze with light. Hettie grabbed her briefcase, jumped out and locked the car.

This would be one meeting none of them would ever forget.

Chapter Eleven

"I'm so thankful to the Goddess you are all here tonight." Hettie stood in the middle of Darla's family room, not knowing where or how to begin.

Darla rose from the small couch and put an arm around her, gave her a squeeze. "Start at the beginning."

Ella patted the seat Darla had vacated. "Come, sit by me. We're your coven. There's not anything you can't share with us."

Mae, the crone of their small group, sat on the recliner.

Young Ivy sat cross-legged on the carpet munching on a bowl of popcorn.

Rosalba paced the room a bundle of nervous energy. "Leah, my spiritual guide, came to me earlier today. She told me of dark arts being practiced here in our town, directly related to you, Hettie." She crossed her arms and narrowed her eyes at Hettie. "Are you involved in this evil?"

If looks could kill, Hettie would have been lying on the carpet taking her last breath. Her heart shuddered, for she had brought this danger to her friends. Not intentionally, and yet, she felt responsible. Declan was here in the present because of his obsession with her.

"Please, Rosalba, sit down," Hettie said. "I have a story to tell you. I never had amnesia."

"Go on, child," Mae said. She waved her hand in Rosalba's direction. "Sit. Hettie is going to tell us her story. No more interruptions."

Rosalba plopped down on the brown overstuffed chair.

Hettie gathered her courage. "Difficult as it is to believe, I've time traveled from the year sixteen-ninety-two."

A collective gasp filled the air.

"Cool!" Ivy said. "Don't start till I get back." She'd polished off the popcorn and returned the empty bowl to the kitchen.

Darla stood with her spirit staff and then tapped the stick three times on the floor. "I call our coven to order. I evoked a protection spell on my house earlier. I thought it prudent after Rosalba told me of the black magick. Whatever we hear or say will be kept within these walls. Hettie, you may begin"

"I was born Henrietta Anne Wynn on October first in sixteen-seventy-four." She went on to tell them everything so they would be prepared for the battle to come.

Hettie finished her story by saying, "And Declan showed up at The Crystal Witch this evening. I've got to stop him. He's evil. I have no idea how he got here or if he's going back. I know I'm asking lot, but I need your help. I can't fight him alone."

Rosalba was the first to reach Hettie, embracing her in a hug. "You poor girl. What you've been through. I'm with you whatever we have to do."

Everyone jumped at the ding-dong of the doorbell. "Probably the pizza I ordered," Darla laughed and went to answer the door. She peeked out the window before removing the protection spell.

"Hey, what are you doing here? I'm glad to see you, but our coven is meeting tonight, cousin."

"Is Hettie here? I've just come from her shop. It looks like a bomb exploded inside." Evan's voice cut through Hettie's thoughts.

"Evan, I'm in here. How did you know where to find me?" Relief flooded through her.

He stood in the living room and removed his scarf and jacket. He only had eyes for Hettie.

"I figured Ella might know, and when she wasn't home I remembered Darla had a meeting tonight, thought Ella would be here." He ran his hands through his hair, "I went by your shop. It was a mess. Soap or something all over the floor, shelves ripped down. The whole shop was a disaster and the front door was off the hinges. What the hell happened?" His eyes blazed like black embers.

Ella got up off the sofa.

"Sit, Evan. I've a story to tell you and it is long." Hettie took his hand and led the way to the couch. "It's time to tell you who I really am."

Chapter Twelve

Hettie finished her story and said, "I'll understand, Evan, if you don't want to see me anymore."

"Quit seeing you? When I've just found you?" He pulled Hettie into his embrace. "I'll protect you with everything I've got. I can't lose you. Not now, somehow you've become part of my heart and I'm not giving you up, my love."

Hettie's heart filled with joy. Instead of running for the hills, Evan vowed to protect her.

"I am not Waya, but I am descended from the same ancestors. The same blood flows through my veins that flowed through Waya's." Reaching under his shirt collar he brought forth a bone moon on a leather thong. A matching one to the one Waya had given her.

She reached beneath her top and pulled forth the matching one. "Together, forever."

He leaned down and kissed her. "Together, forever."

The coven cheered and formed a circle around the couple. Love was a strong binding agent.

Individually they would be no match for Declan, but with six witches and Evan, they might stand a chance. In a way, she guessed Waya had found her.

It turned out Evan, like his cousin, Darla Blackfeather had some magick powers inherited from their tribal ancestors.

Everyone contributed to the plan to defeat Declan. The ritual would take place on Samhain, four days from now.

Hettie parked her car behind the shop. Evan pulled in behind her, and then Ella's BMW with the other five witches inside. Hettie walked into the shop with the others behind her. She stopped, aghast;

the shelves were back up on the walls, the broken items mended and the soaps back on the table in their pretty handmade wrappers. The door creaked, still hanging by one hinge. The rest had been restored to look as it had this morning when she opened up the shop.

"How is this possible?" Hettie looked at the witches.

"While you told Evan about your story, I snuck out and worked a little magick." Ella toyed with her blonde ponytail.

"Thanks, but what about the sheriff?"

"He won't remember the phone call. I didn't think it wise for him to know about Declan." Ella grabbed up the teapot and headed for the sink. "Don't worry, I erased the 9-1-1 call from the on-call dispatcher's memory, and anyone who saw the shop in disarray will not hold the memory of the incident."

"Do you have a toolbox?" Evan shoved his hands in his pockets.

"Yes, in the office on the floor behind the desk." Warmed by Ella's thoughtfulness, Hettie smiled.

Carrying a screw driver he walked over and fixed the door. He shut the door firmly, secured the lock, and pulled down the shade.

"What are you doing, Ella? It's late. You should all go home." Hettie had to let out a little breath at the happiness in her heart; these were her friends and they cared what happened to her. They had more than proved to be gray witches and willing to join forces with her to fight Declan.

"Hettie's right. You can go home." Evan slipped his arm around Hettie's waist and pulled her close. "I'll be with her tonight."

Hettie felt the surge of energy that followed any contact with Evan.

Darla exchanged a look of "I told you so!" with Ella. "That's fine if you stay with her, but we'll be invoking protection and security spells down here," Darla said. "Declan can't get upstairs unless Hettie invites him. He can create mayhem in the shop, unless we put these in place." She shook her finger at Evan. "There's no changing our minds. Off with the two of you. Being in love, having love and making love are three of the most powerful elements against evil that exist."

Ella gave a shooing motion with her hand. "Off with you!"

Behind them Ivy, Mae and Rosalba chanted a spell in unison three times.

Sleep safe this night, the two of you.
Love surround and protect thee,
Fuse this love that is so new,
So mote it be.

Hettie hesitated with her hand on the doorknob to her apartment. No one had ever entered her sanctuary. She trusted Evan. She felt safe and cared for, and even loved when she was near him. Her sexual awakening was in no small part due to this man. Along with her heightened senses of magick. Since meeting him she had a greater awareness of her strength, her magick powers.

Kitty waited patiently on the landing. Hettie picked him up and stroked the fuzzy orange cat. She spoke the opening charm and entered her room. With a flick of her hand, the Tiffany lamp turned on, the shades closed and soft lovely music of violins played in the background. She set Kitty down on the floor and he jumped up on the rocking chair.

Evan turned her around and touched his forehead to hers. "Hettie, we'll get through this together. I'll sleep on the couch."

She unzipped his jacket, pushed it down his arms. She wanted, needed this man. "No floor for you tonight." She took his hand and led him to the bed.

With another wave of her hand, the lamp clicked off and a dozen candles throughout the room flamed to life. She took off her clothes and stood before him in only her bra and lace panties. Magick and love flowed through her.

He worked fast to strip down, comically hopping on one foot to get his last sock off.

As she reached for her hair clip, Evan caught her wrist. "Let me. I've wanted to take that clip out since the first day I met you." He undid the clip, and finger combed her hair till it hung in long curls down her back to her waist. "Beautiful. Your hair, your body, your soul…." He cupped her chin and kissed her sweetly on the lips. He slipped one finger under the strap on her bra followed it to her back and unclasped it. Then he slid her lacey underwear down. The burning in her belly threatened to consume her; she couldn't wait any longer. She pulled him down on the bed with her, kissing him with all the built up passion she had.

"Is this what you want, Hettie?" His voice husky with pent up desire.

"I'm sure. Stop talking." She pulled him down on top. Skin to skin didn't cause electric shocks instead their touching made magick. She was vaguely aware of the bed rising off the ground like a wonderful cloud floating in her room. Stars sparkled on the ceiling and the music reached a crescendo each time they climaxed. Evan made love to her three times during the night. Their destiny was sealed. He was hers and she was his. The strongest union between a man and a woman, Gram's tome said, was a bond of love.

Chapter Thirteen

Time flew by, and the eve of Samhain arrived. Each time Hettie looked out her window at the woods she felt a dark energy. Declan was near, just biding his time. The protection spells had worked. Tonight Ella and Darla would remove the spells before leaving for the sacred circle. Hettie dressed in her black wool dress, black boots and shawl, the same ones she had worn when she arrived in this time period.

When she entered the shop to see Ella and Darla in their witch's costumes, she had to chuckle. They looked beautiful and deadly at the same time. They were helping her with the shop this evening. Evan was Paul Bunyan, complete with an axe and horn handled knife on his belt. He had told Hettie the knife had been passed down to each Shaman through the ages. At one time Waya had possessed it.

"You all look great," Hettie said.

"Come see the children," Ella gushed. "They are all so darn cute!"

Hettie hurried toward the door, grabbing her witch's hat off the counter.

"Trick or treat!" said a little devil accompanied by a tiny witch and a zombie.

"Oh, blessed be!" Hettie took three little crystal witches and blessed each one before dropping them into the Halloween sacks.

"Thank you," they said in unison.

"Sorry I missed most of the trick-or-treaters," Hettie told her friends. "I was reworking my spell and getting things together for the circle." Mentally she checked off her list: spell, broom, crystal wand, bowl for water, black ribbon, and a sprig of rosemary. Blessed be to the Goddess for giving her the fortitude to start work on the spell last year. The spell to travel into the past would be used tonight to send Declan back through time.

"Do you think this Declan will show up?" Darla asked.

"He will. He wants me and he wants my power. The hardest part will be convincing him I'll go along." A cold wind blew through the store despite the closed door and windows. "Declan. He's near."

"Evan, can you take Ella and Darla to meet the others, by the old hemlock tree, the one near the sacred circle?" Hettie withdrew her crystal wand and the written spell from her bag of tools and handed her bag to Ella. She had memorized the spell. She put the slip of paper in her pocket for safekeeping.

"You sure you want me to leave?" his voice husky with concern.

"Yes. We must all stick to the plan. And thank all of you for your support."

Hettie took hold of Ella's free hand and grabbed Darla's hand. "Ella and Darla sweep the sacred circle, prepare it, and thank you both so much for helping. I... ." For a long moment she looked at Evan. "We couldn't do it without you."

After the others left, Hettie sat waiting. Her mind reviewed all the ways this could go terribly wrong. She shook herself; positive thoughts only. Tired of sitting and tired of waiting, she paced to the front of the store and back, again and again.

Evan would build a fire outside the circle. Fire was a powerful protector and as long as he stayed by it, he should be safe. The fire was important too, because after the incantation was cast, she needed to burn the written spell. The ashes would consummate the spell and seal the incantation. Once burnt, it could never be revoked.

The door to the shop opened. "Hello, Henrietta." Declan's voice was clear and crisp as a frosty morning. He moved toward her with a slow predatory stride.

She could do this, she could do this. She repeated her mantra. "Declan, you came back." Goose bumps scurried across skin so cold even her wool dress failed to warm her.

"How quaint, you kept your dress. But then it is only fitting you go back in time in what you wore when you left. My, my, do you have to stoop to playing the part? You look magnificent without this ridiculous hat." He took the witch hat off her head tossing it on the table He strode to the back of the shop, checking in the storeroom. "No one here just you and me. How delightful!"

She was keenly aware of his scrutiny. He looked her over, circling her, and she stood perfectly still, not moving an inch for fear of his retribution. She prayed to the Goddess Evan and the other witches were at the circle now, preparing for the battle to come; if only she knew they were safe for sure. She needed to stick to the plan and get Declan to the Sacred Circle.

"Aren't you happy to see me?" Declan drew a finger down her cheek across her lip, down her neck, and encircled her neck with his hand. "Ready to give yourself to me of your own free will, as promised?" He tightened his hold on her neck and cut off her oxygen. She convulsed in a fit of coughing and he eased up.

Hettie shrugged loose and stepped away, rubbing her sore neck. "Only on my own terms. Only if we go back to Waxing as it was, to Waya, to that night when I left."

Declan chuckled. "Ah-h I suppose you wish to see your Indian lover once more. You know he died trying to save his father. Heroic till the minute my knife stopped his beating heart. All for the best; he would have died of a broken heart had he lived."

He grabbed her arm in a painful hold, pulling her to within inches of his face. "Kiss me Henrietta, show me you've changed. When we are joined, there'll be no stopping what we can do. Our power will rule the world. Kiss me!"

The plan, she had to stick to the plan. She was drawn to him, a spell he had invoked, surely. Summoning her power, she put up a wall against his bewitchments. She wouldn't kiss him. She pulled away, backing toward the door. "No, 'tis enough I've agreed to go with you."

"I'll taste your treats later. The woods haven't changed much. Some trees fallen and are gone from the landscape, I was pleased to find the old hemlock tree. It's definitely full of magick. It could sense me." He fluttered his fingers. "The needles on the old tree quivered when I walked by." He advanced on her. "And your pathetic excuse for a Sacred Circle. Really, Henrietta, I expected you to create a more powerful circle, not use such a primitive one. However, as it turns out I came through the veil at nearly the same location."

Grabbing her and bending her arm behind her, he aimed her out the back door.

Chapter Fourteen

"What's this?" Declan said. "This little gang of witches believes they're going to stop me? Ha!" He pushed Hettie so hard she stumbled. Jerking her back against him, Declan pulled out his ritual knife, and laid the blade against her neck. Warmth oozed a trail down her neck. Declan had nicked her!

Evan's eyes snapped midnight black completely focused on Declan. He clenched his fists. Declan maneuvered Hettie into the center of the circle.

Stick to the plan, Hettie telepathed to Evan. When his eyes locked with hers she knew he heard.

Hettie felt the trickle of warm blood on her neck. Evan wouldn't want to give Declan any reason to slice her deeper. The five witches touched fingertip to fingertip, completing a circle around Declan and Hettie. They moved counter clockwise and lifted their arms skyward.

Ella led the chant as they moved around the circle:
Earth, Air, Fire, Water circle round,
Hold this space, this hallowed ground.

Darla led the next chant:

East, south, west, north,
Goddess, listen to your daughters.
The third time around, all the witches chanted:
Bring power forth!

The circle of witches floated free of the ground. The chanting had changed to the old tongue. Hettie saw Evan slip his Shaman knife from the scabbard.

The magick directed at Declan was so intense he dropped his knife. Now the knife lay in a molten pile of metal. He spun Hettie around to face him and grabbed her wrists. His eyes flashed in anger. "You will come with me!" Declan's voice rose to a devilish pitch as he spoke the ancient words. Binding words.

Hettie prayed to the Goddess.

Would her coven and Evan be enough?

Colored spheres of lights filled the circle, as well as smoke and haze, and through it all, Hettie was aware of Evan. She threw back her head, her face to the sky she shut her eyes, and uttered the words over and over in the language of ancient magick.

She opened her eyes. Evan crouched by the circle, knife ready. Declan's eyes were orbs of red and he chanted faster, and faster.

The other witches spun around her and Declan. The passionate heat from all the magick was powerful.

Hettie locked in an embrace with Declan. They were starting to spin a foot off the ground. She spoke the words, freed her hands and tied the black ribbon around Declan's wrist. She held the other end chanting the final spell:

> *I tie to your wrist the ribbon of magick;*
> *So Declan you know what I have done.*
> *And when this ribbon touches two;*
> *It's what matters,*
> *When the ribbon is cut in two*
> *The curse is shattered,*
> *Along with you!*
> *So mote it be.*

Evan rushed into the circle and sliced through the ribbon. A powerful *whoosh* blew through the circle and the swirling light disappeared.

The witches were back on the ground, encircling Hettie and Evan. Declan had disappeared.

"We did it, he's gone! We did it!" Ella laughed. "He's really gone."

"That was pure awesomeness!" Ivy declared.

Darla patted the sweat from her forehead with the hem of her dress. "I thought we were going to be roasted!"

Hettie slowly turned around and captured Evan's eyes. She held the crystal wand, which glowed with charged energy. Blood continued to drip down her neck. "Evan?"

He scooped her up and carried her to a stump where he sat, cradling her. He took his Paul Bunyan kerchief off and dabbed up the blood. "You were fantastic, my crystal witch. What a show, ladies — it was spectacular. Is Declan gone for good?"

"The spell! Quick we must burn it!" Hettie dug in her pocket and produced the piece of paper.

"I'll take that, child," Mae said. She rested heavily on her cane. The crone carried the written spell to the bonfire and held it over the flames. She held the paper till only a slip remained and then dropped the remaining bit into the blaze.

Evan kissed Hettie long and passionately. "No more secrets. Did you send me a telepathic message?"

"I was sure you heard me." Hettie smiled. "You are my true love."

"As you are mine." His voice was low and seductive, and held all the promise of an enchanted life together.

"Yes, always and forever!" Joy bubbled in her laugh.

THE END